THE CAT AT LIGHT'S END

and other stories

Charlie Dickinson

lulu.com
2004

Copyright 2004 by Charlie Dickinson

All rights reserved. No part of this book may be reproduced in any manner without the express consent of the author, except in the case of brief excerpts in critical reviews and articles.

Acknowledgements

I am grateful to the following online publications where these stories originally appeared: *Amarillo Bay*: "La Mosca" and "The President, He Slept Here." *Blue Moon Review*: "Marbles on the Loose." *Eclectica*: "The Cat at Light's End." *InterText*: "Espresso'd." *Mississippi Review*: "Steps." *News From the Brave New World*: "Cydney's Bent," "Fear & Trembling," and "Red Ball." *Savoy*: "Past Perfect," "Talking Cabbage Heads," "Timed Out," and "Zigzag." *Southern Cross Review*: "Valentines in Valhalla."

~~CD

For Nancia

Contents

The Cat at Light's End   1
Zigzag   13
Fear & Trembling   25
Marbles on the Loose   41
The President, He Slept Here   57
Valentines in Valhalla   67
Red Ball   81
Timed Out   91
La Mosca   103
Talking Cabbage Heads   117
Past Perfect   123
Cydney's Bent   131
Espresso'd   145
Steps   157

THE CAT AT LIGHT'S END

Jayne knew exactly how she, Russ, their daughter Alyssa, and a cat ended up living out of a beater Econoline van, now parked at a Fred Meyer's One-Stop Shopping Center in Portland, Oregon. It was as obvious, as unavoidable, once things were in motion, as a good car wreck. Some six months ago, things got tough when Nehalem Lumber laid off Russ and all the other mill workers.

Nothing Russ or anybody did. The word was simply "No more logs to cut."

Jayne saw Russ and his buddies try as they may to keep each other up with jokes about tree huggers and owls. He put a bumper sticker on the Econoline: ARE YOU AN ENVIRONMENTALIST OR DO YOU WORK FOR A LIVING? Russ's buddies got a kick out of that one.

But Jayne realized the growing truth of a mill that would never reopen was bearing down. They scraped by with money from unemployment. Russ even admitted that because he was out of work, he should take off the bumper sticker. Then he got madder about bureaucrats stealing their way of life and decided the bumper sticker would stay.

Weeks rolled by. The owl jokes got scarcer and what Jayne heard out of Russ was talk about buddies moving on. Some set off for Seattle to drive trucks at good pay, bach'ing it until their families could come up for more permanent arrangements.

Things, though, would not turn for Russ. And when they wanted to have a garage sale and raise money, they discovered

Vernonia had too many garage sales and too many people holding cash tight. One thing led to another. They gave away most of their junk, kept a few good things with Russ's brother, and then, a few weeks back, with the rent due, took up life in the van.

Jayne lit one of her cigarettes, the Virginia Slims she called Ginny Skinnies. She did not mind the waiting. Who knows? Russ *could* get on at Fred Meyer's.

Back of the front seat in the Econoline, Alyssa screamed Toby scratched her, but Jayne knew a scrawny kitten was not up to scratching anybody. "Alys*sa*," she said in a voice wise to kid tricks. Toby had escaped into the plaid flannel liner of one of the two green sleeping bags.

Jayne let it be and looked over the sorry, plain apartments just outside the parking lot. Did people living there have any idea how quick their personal situation might just sour and leave them out on the street? She took a long drag, then lowered her eyes and blew a smoke ring with her lips *O*'d-out like a hungry fish.

Alyssa giggled, then tried to stop, without much success. She was being bad. Jayne raised her cigarette, gave her four-year-old the eye.

Alyssa had Toby up on his hind legs. The light-colored fur on his chest and belly showed more than the darker tabby stripes. Poor Toby looked like some Muppet she wanted to make dance.

Jayne stubbed the cigarette in the ashtray.

"Alyssa, put him down, right this second. Now!" What was it with kids that made them enjoy torturing animals?

"Mommy, I'm not hurting him," Alyssa said softly like she might get spanked. "Toby wants to play." She started to smooth the fur on his back, but he crawled away for the other side of the van.

"Give him here," Jayne said. "He probably wants to go and your teasing don't help things one bit." Jayne winced at the idea of cat pee on sleeping bags. Would that smell ever hang around for a while.

Alyssa flopped over, grabbing the cat by the tail like she was in a game of tackle football.

"Alyssa, watch yourself—he's going to take a leak!"

Jayne took Toby in hand, pushed open the door, got out, and plunked him down on the blacktop. His spindly legs made him look unsteady. He sniffed the pavement. Jayne got a handful of cat litter and tossed it well under the van. She didn't need Russ yapping about stepping in a cat's little puddle.

"Whatcha doin'? Whatcha doin'?"

"This primes the pump," Jayne said, then she picked up Toby and slid his spindly legs smack in the middle of the cat litter. He stood still, then scratched with a forepaw. Alyssa hung out the door, head upside down to see everything.

"Alyssa, get back in the car." Toby was pawing to cover up a patch of damp cat litter.

Before Toby could walk anywhere, Jayne grabbed and tossed him on the sleeping bags. Alyssa took him in her arms.

"I love you, kitty. Don't ever leave me like Figaro. Poor Figaro."

They found old Figaro lying on the back steps, flies all over his head. Jayne told Alyssa he had gone to heaven where every cat is happy. Didn't matter. Alyssa cried she would never have another cat so special.

That is, until Toby a month ago. Toby was free and came with markings just like Figaro.

"Uh, oh," Jayne said, "doesn't look like Daddy's got good news."

Head down, Russ walked back to the van with a bunch of papers.

"How'd it go?" Jayne asked.

Russ pulled himself up to a full six-foot-two and shook the papers like he just might throw them away. "Oh, nice guy and all, wants me to fill these out even though he doesn't have any current openings and nothing coming up." He gazed skyward.

Jayne got another cigarette going. "Oh, sure," she said, her words mixed with smoke, "like on the off-chance he's got some dork in mind he's set to fire any day." Jayne kept an eye on Alyssa.

"Right. Sounds like a line he's paid to tell anyone comes in for employment." His words trailed off.

"Daddy's getting a jo-*ob*," Alyssa said to Toby all singsongy. She had him dancing on his hind legs again.

"Did you tell him you wanted to work produce?" Jayne asked.

"You bet. First thing I said. But he said most likely any opening's gonna be bottle returns."

"Bottle returns!"

"That's what I thought. Then I asked him what the pay was, how many hours, I couldn't believe it."

"That job's for a kid living at home."

"Yeah. I came right out and said no way could I feed a wife and kid and live any place half decent here in Portland."

"And little Toby!" Alyssa cried out.

"I don't know," Russ said. "That little kitty might have to go out for his own dinner this situation don't pick up."

"Mommy, you said we'd keep Toby." Alyssa looked at Toby's golden eyes. "You said he was for me. You did."

"Alys*sa*," Jayne said, "that's not what Daddy meant. He just meant we might have to find someone to take Toby in if we can't feed him. That's all."

Alyssa's face twisted with pain as if she knew Russ was really thinking about dumping her cat at the pound.

"No, no, Toby's mine. I'll always take care of him." She was crying.

"A cat? That's the least of our worries," Russ said to Jayne.

Alyssa sobbed tears that got her face good and red. She gasped for breath and blurted out, "Toby's mine. We'll run away. We'll live in the forest." Jayne reached one hand back as if to comfort her, then glanced sideways at Russ.

He had out the electric blue nylon wallet and tore back the Velcro flap stained with grease. "Look, this is it, not even one hundred fifty." Russ thumbed the twenties, the fives, the ones. He slapped the wallet shut. Alyssa got quiet. "This is it. Spend it on food and gas and there's nothing more. So if that cat's gotta go, it's because he's taking chances like all of us."

He grabbed the bag with Toby's food and asked how many cat food cans were left. He ignored Alyssa hugging Toby. Russ counted cans. "Five more days, Toby, you're on your own."

Jayne turned away from Russ. Stared again at the apartments. Why did he single out Toby? And five days? A hundred fifty's not gonna let the rest of them eat much longer. A month, if that. Russ was not in a good mood. She would keep her thoughts private.

They stopped at a pay phone by a gas station. Russ had focus. He copied out addresses for another Fred Meyer, some Safeways, and an Albertson's, all on the Eastside. Jayne did not see what it was with grocery stores. He could cast in different waters. But Russ knew what he wanted: "Produce, not bottle returns." He said it was a matter of saying the same line over and over. Somewhere, some grocery store had to buy the pitch and take him on.

Jayne wanted to tell Russ to apply some place that advertised openings, but then buried in the van was a family heirloom. A pickled thumb from one of Russ's uncles. He axed it off on a dare. Russ could have inherited a genetics problem about not letting go of a challenge. Anyway, Jayne understood, had no advice, especially with how Russ felt about Toby.

So in a parking lot, out a parking lot, the Econoline went and they hit a total of five stores for the afternoon. While they waited at each stop, Alyssa went back to teasing Toby. The shrieks and questions were such that Jayne promised her she could suggest one thing for dinner. At Albertson's, Russ returned to say, "There's only so much rejection a guy can take."

"You made it through your list of stores," Jayne said.

"And I'm beat as a broken drum."

Jayne glanced at store shoppers coming out the automatic doors, pushing loaded carts. "Hate to mention it," Jayne said, "but this place as good as any to get some things for dinner."

Russ folded his arms on the steering wheel and rested his head.

"I wouldn't make you do that. I'll go in," Jayne said.

Alyssa jumped, holding on the seatback. "Potato chips, mommy, potato chips."

They headed over to Forest Park where tall fir trees kept things well in the shade except where sunlight sparkled off a playground slide, a pair of swings, and a merry-go-round, which had a real circle of a rut from kids running next to it.

Alyssa wanted someone to push her on a swing. Jayne sighed. Who could blame the kid cooped up in the van all day? But Russ said first came dinner. Jayne made tuna-and-mustard sandwiches and they broke open the bag of chips and with Pepsi from a 32-ounce plastic bottle, they washed it all down.

After the food was gone, Russ asked Alyssa if she was ready for the swings.

"What's for dessert," she said, then giggled.

"Young lady," Russ said, as if holding back a spanking, "you better be thankful, you got to eat."

"She is, Russ. You saw she ate most of the potato chips." Jayne tied off in its plastic bag what was left of the bread, wondering how to use it for breakfast tomorrow.

Alyssa giggled.

Russ kneeled and brushed his daughter's bangs away from her forehead. "You think she enjoys being a pest?" he said to Jayne.

"No, I'm not," Alyssa said. She put hands on hips, elbows out.

"Then let's see you over on the swings."

Before long, Russ was pushing Alyssa in the swing so far off the ground, she laughed nonstop. She shrieked. Jayne remembered Alyssa could be fun when she was good.

Jayne tossed the trash. What could tomorrow bring? It had been one discouraging day for Russ.

After Alyssa tired of the swing, the merry-go-round, and the slide, they sat around the table and fed Toby dinner and told stories about when things were easier back in Vernonia. The cat licked his fur, cleaning himself. The sky went dark like the shadows around them. With the four of them at the picnic table, Jayne felt for a moment oddly happy, remembering they were a family, forgetting they were living out of a van.

The park was empty and Alyssa was half-asleep against Jayne. Russ yawned.

Jayne carried Alyssa over to the Econoline and Russ followed with Toby. After some tired words, they were ready for the sack.

In the morning, Jayne woke to the sight of Toby curled up on the dashboard. His fur seemed almost on fire in morning light. Jayne studied the glow about Toby. She had slept really well. She was so rested that she did not feel like having a smoke or feel like she needed coffee just yet.

Toby's tail twitched like he was in a dream. How could he know he had five days of food left?

Jayne could see that Toby acted as if things would turn out okay. He had no sense of how tomorrow things could get bad. The sun was there keeping him warm. What else did he need to know?

Jayne knew things would be okay for them too. Toby would keep them going.

Russ zipped himself out of the sleeping bag. His tousled hair needed combing, his stubbly whiskers, shaving. She could kid him about applying for a job looking like that, but she wouldn't. On the front seat, Alyssa slept on, one side of her face reddened with crease lines from the upholstery where she'd turned over.

Jayne wanted to untangle the small blanket about her feet, but it was no use waking her.

"Look at that. Asleep," Jayne whispered to Russ when he straightened up for a look, mostly out of habit, at his daughter. "She was so upset yesterday. Hard to believe it's the same girl."

"Upset about what?" Russ locked eyes with Jayne like he was trying to figure how much argument was on tap. "You startin' in on the cat again."

"Russ, I'm sorry. But I've decided we're gonna keep Toby. Come hell, come high water. We're gonna keep him. I'm sorry."

"Sorry, she says. Sorry is another mouth to feed." Russ whipped closed the top flap of the sleeping bag, his face settled down to a good crabbed look. Jayne eyed Toby. His fur had stopped glowing from the sun. She needed to calm down; she wanted a cigarette. "What do we have?" Russ said. "Six dollars less than I counted out yesterday."

"Wait a minute," she said. "That cat never ate through fifty cents worth of food any day of his life. So what's the six dollars? Besides, that's not the problem. Problem's Alyssa thinks you're gonna take Toby to the pound so they'll put him to sleep." She took a slow, deep breath. Russ could get her mad, she'd let him.

"She didn't get that idea from me. Personally, I don't believe in pounds. Set him free on some back road, he'll survive in the wild—"

"Survive in the wild—you think we can?"

"What do you mean by that?" Russ seemed as confused as some parachutist in a tree.

"Toby no more gonna survive in the wild than we can. You know that, Russ. If he's done for, we're done for. Admit it."

"That the way you want to see it, okay. The money runs out, we're all done for. So?"

"I was just thinking we're all in this together." The sleeping form on the front seat started to stir. "We can't stop feeding Toby anymore we can stop feeding Alyssa or any of us." Jayne thought it was cute how Alyssa would keep her eyes shut, the rest of her moving, when she awoke. "And you gotta hang on to hope that things will turn." She pinched the toes of one foot, suddenly remembering past times she'd enjoy putting coral polish on her toenails. Not any more.

"You gonna give that cat a tin cup?"

"Okay, you keep it up, Mr. Smarty Pants Sad Sack. Let Alyssa and I be positive. We know there's a job here in Portland. Russ is written on it in neon letters—" Jayne smiled at Russ like they could have been the oldest of friends.

"Stop it, you're wishful thinking on me. That job sure ain't got no Fred Meyer neon letters."

Her face sweaty and flush, Alyssa pulled herself up on the front seat. Her eyes were opened wide like she was lost in the forest, running from that fairy-tale gingerbread house. "Mommy, they were after me. I couldn't run. My legs wouldn't move. I was so scared, Mommy."

Russ's eyes cut to his daughter with a peevish gaze. "That's all those potato chips," Jayne said softly. "You ate too many potato chips last night, Alyssa. Your blood gets agitated, then you get nightmares." Even Jayne could believe that, or maybe it was that she felt hungry for some good food and a smoke afterward. "Say, I have an idea. Let's eat breakfast at a real restaurant."

"What and starve a day sooner?"

"No, over at Newberry's. I saw the sign we drove by yesterday. Breakfast, dollar forty-nine. Two eggs, bacon, toast, coffee. What do you say? It's their come-on special for us folks that are economical."

Russ dropped back his head and gave the torn headliner in the van a quizzical look before he said anything. "I have a choice?"

Jayne figured a man's stomach knows when to stop arguing. "And we could get Alyssa a glass of milk and give her some of our toast."

"We keep him," Russ said, flagging an index finger at Toby, "he better not bring me bad luck, all I have to say."

At Newberry's, the three sat in a row at an old-style counter, its shiny aluminum edging hugging the Formica top. The waiter, an older fellow with a gray crewcut, wore a black-and-white checked shirt under a white kitchen apron. After toweling off the counter, he hesitated about where the towel went, then he gave them breakfast menus with enough awkwardness that Jayne guessed he was covering for someone who was late for work.

Russ went ahead, ordered. Two of the dollar forty-nine specials and a glass of milk, which the stand-in waiter got down on an order pad. "Will that be all?" he asked, eyeing Alyssa, who was busy unpacking and sorting every jam packet from a counter bowl. Jayne thought better of telling him that Alyssa would share their toast.

Right when the waiter was about to clip the order on the carousel for the cook, Russ stopped scratching his chin and called out, "One other thing, I almost forgot, we'd like a side order of crispy fried spotted owl wings to go."

"Maybe we should put that on the menu," the waiter said. Russ's eyes twinkled like he'd found a timber buddy.

"Russ," Jayne said, "this is not Vernonia."

He palmed Alyssa's shoulder. "I can't say threatening things about her four-legged friend, I gotta unleash a crack or two about Mr. Who Who." Alyssa said the orange marmalades were first and slowly pushed the other jam packets aside. The waiter returned with two coffees and then fetched a glass of milk and a straw.

And minutes later, he brought two plates with the breakfasts and offered to get ketchup or Tabasco. "No," Jayne said, "but can I trouble you for an extra plate. My daughter, she sometimes gets messy." Alyssa wiggled away Jayne's knife.

The waiter studied Alyssa, the four orange marmalade packets she'd piled up on the counter. "Sure thing," the waiter said. "How about an order of toast on that plate?"

"No, she's got enough with milk."

"Today's manager special. Extra toast on a double breakfast order." He clasped his two hands together like he would be ready with the toast in a jiff.

"No charge?" Jayne had to be sure.

"No charge. What do you want, Miss: white or wheat?"

"White toast," Alyssa said and he went to get the toast and Jayne took a sip of her coffee, blonde with real half-and-half. Why was her squirmy daughter so behaved in public? Maybe thanks to this man who knew a small kid wants her own toast, even when the parents have to watch their money, even when the picky eater is likely to eat no more than half a slice of bread.

With a few people here, there like the waiter, Jayne saw the city could, like Vernonia, be home. Once they stopped living in the van. The van where they still had to feed Toby what little food he really needed. Worse came to worse, she could pick up pop cans and beer bottles for that money. Russ was mopping his egg with toast. She knew he'd come around and not be so choosy about what job he wanted—then he'd get a bounce his way. Jayne knew that as live truth. And, hot damn, the owl jokes were back.

ZIGZAG

What at first was an ordinary cool, moonlit night, a fog came and smothered. A drastic fog, it climbed the banks of the Willamette River to roll across, to take and hide the Irvington Neighborhood, where a block away from storefront glare and crawling traffic on Broadway, apartment two-stories lined the next street, Schuyler. A cabdriver there, early on the pickup, stretched his legs, conceding the weather had slowed him down, would cut his pay for the night. He rested on the right front fender, gave hawkish attention for anyone leaving Tillamook Court. Behind him, the dome light emblazing ROY'S CAB CALL 555-1212 seemed likely to attract nothing more than weepy fog.

    The building door opened. A tall woman, lean—the cabby guessed her a looker up close—paused, clasped her gray overcoat, then left it open. Her wool sweater, which might have been basic black, was more than offset by her pants—blue textured Matka silk that flashed even in the foggy air as she hastened toward the cabby, the sidewalk.

    His wristwatch showed 1:58 am. He unslouched, tugged the brim of his sat-upon cap. "You call for a taxi?"

    The handsome woman, keeping from him the transitory joy of eye contact, turned right. "No, sorry," she said several steps away.

    Her stride was with purpose. This was the last Kim expected to see of her apartment or what went with it. She scowled at the blurry street lights. That cabdriver, Why was he there? Were the gods toying with her again? Checking if she had lost nerve?

They would see. And they would be her only audience—this fog gave such sweet anonymity. She had held back, off and on, for weeks but soon with blissful seconds of wingless flight, pointing her toes—let the gods grade her high on form—it would end.

Yes, the gods saw this coming. They offered her signs all the time. Washing dishes, she would meditate on a sharp knife edge—far too slow, she knew that much—and music on the radio would segue, no pause, to Don McLean's "Starry Night." Poor Vincent. Beautiful, tortured Vincent.

Or she would be at the library picking up a new Grafton for the insomnia. On the bookshelf, completely misplaced, some agent for the gods had left *PDR for Prescription Drugs*.

So for the next half hour, Kim devoured the esoterica of phenobarbital, among other pharmaceutical choices, wondering how she could collect enough pills. And coincidence or not, Kim was now the same age—thirty-six—as Marilyn Monroe when that famed sister joined the exclusive sorority.

Kim shivered. Not that it mattered. She had no need to be warm again. Warm could stay away. All she needed was to walk less than two miles to the Broadway Bridge, where removing shoes she would have a railing to ease over and let go.

Then twenty yards distant, brake lights from the first passing car flared in the tumbling fog. White backup lights, then beside her, a power window came down.

"Excuse me, Miss, the idea of a date tonight fit your schedule?" He clicked on the headliner lamp. The man, older, looked like he could afford the car.

She lowered her head. "No, thanks, I'm out for a walk." She gathered her coat flaps. Was this the last judgment from the relentless gods, this man suggesting she was a whore? The gods got that wrong. She had no use for money, not after tonight.

He seemed to be smiling at the hesitancy she felt standing there, her best silk pants almost garish in the situation. Wearing a jogging suit, he leaned her way in the cream leather seat, arm and hand riding the maple veneer trim. "I got a few hundred dollars, what do you say, we go some place nice?"

This would be her last chance to do sex. And if this guy tested positive on every retrovirus known to man, did it matter? No, not for Ophelia adrift in the Willamette when the sun rose. It didn't matter, not really.

He pinched the remote fob on the ignition key, reached over, inched the door ajar like it was some bank vault.

She was inside.

"No names, please," she said, buckling in. "We don't need names for this." On the cushy leather seat, Kim noted the new car smell. A wedding ring glinted before he snapped off the light. "Nice car," she said.

"Jaguar. New model, leasing gets you in so easily." His face fell into a habitual smile, one that he perhaps had mastered. Kim guessed stockbroker or bank loan officer.

"You mind we run down to QwikBuy? I'm out of cigarettes," he said.

"No."

"I saw you walking back there, thought, Why is she out this late?"

Kim rested her head against the padded door pillar, noted the muted sound, Classical 88.8, what she listened to when she tired of song lyrics.

"Then I rolled down the window, saw your face in all this fog, wondered if I could make you happy."

"Listen, I'm beyond happy, okay?"

"I know a motel over on Sandy. It's clean."

"Take me there."

They eased into the half-empty parking lot. A big yellow, black, and red QwikBuy sign hissed above and cut the fog.

Kim peered inside. "I'm here all the time, stay put."

"Okay, as long as you're not having second thoughts."

"Your brand?"

"Picayune 100s. One pack's fine."

"Any special flavor on condoms?" Her wry smile was equal parts her not caring and the idea of being a step ahead of him.

"Hmmm. Lady's choice." He offered a twenty.

Kim rushed the snacks, candies, aspirin, cough drops to a corner shelf with its yin-yang combo of tampons and condoms.

Vikings. Nippled reservoir, no blowing off the sheath. Kim left those alone. Who would want a boring hydraulic engineer's latex fantasy?

She grabbed another box. Pyramids. Flat black latex. Sexy, but odd.

Put them back. The choices. Ribbed and colored. Lubricated plain. Lubricated with spermicide.

Sheers, "The next best thing to nothing at all." Those she took.

The cashier, she had seen elsewhere. Tall, outdoorsy, over-the-collar nutmeg hair. She glanced at the Jag. Her companion seemed troubled.

"This," she said, package of Sheers on the counter. "And one pack Picayune 100s." Then Kim remembered. The parked van on Weidler weeks ago. This cashier guy, arms on the passenger-side window, talking with, she must have been his wife. The guy's facial stubble, how he dressed did not fool Kim—they lived out of the van.

He gave Kim a slow count on the change, like he was new to the employ of QwikBuy. Kim wanted to imagine him happy. She knew better.

They checked into The Breakers, a utility motel out on Sandy Boulevard. The night clerk, a Sikh with a flawlessly tied white turban crowning his thin dark face and darker beard, asked if adult movies might be of interest. Kim's companion answered no and paid the thirty-five in cash.

In room 104, he dead-bolted the door, skinned the cellophane from the cigarette pack, lit up, and then in the lone Naugahyde chair sat, moving nothing more than hand and cigarette.

She shrugged off her coat.

He stared. With an exhibitionist's appetite, Kim unclasped the silk pants and steadying herself, one hand on the dead TV, slipped them from her lithe legs.

Her unsmiling companion sucked and blew from the Picayune lodged in his fingers.

A drafty chill snuck over her skin and she longed to be warm in bed, body on body, fast-bound for a leg-shuddering climax.

But for now she had to be this stripper. In the orangy light, his eyes did no more than climb her legs and fasten on the mystery of the lacy white keystone at the confluence of her thighs. She did not have all night and pulled the sweater over her head, tossed it, and shook her hair.

"Well, you going to do anything besides smoke?" Kim was down to teddy and panties. "I didn't come here for goose bumps."

He crushed the cigarette to a disfigured butt. "Listen, maybe you'll think I'm crazy, but how are you with just talking. I'll still give you two hundred."

Her jaw slackened. She studied him hard. So much for the promise of that arty Jaguar the other side of the hollow door, its engine ticking away, cooling down.

"Oh, a sense of humor, these gods, I'm with a eunuch."

"I don't mean anything personal, I just feel like talking."

"I could be doing better things."

"What?" He flared up another cigarette. "Out walking in the fog, mulling things over."

Kim slipped in the bed, side nearest him, pulling a thin blanket over her legs. She pushed her hair back with both hands and scowled. "I've given up on thinking."

He tapped the cigarette pack, held it out. She had quit more than a year ago, but it did not really matter. She imbibed the Zippo flame, took a short drag, let the smoke play at her throat and nostrils, then leak out.

"So tell me, your tramp steamer of worry, what's it called?"

"Oh, reasons a guy my age stays awake at night."

"Reasons being?"

"Well, my business partner is a crook. Have to engineer our parting without it costing me everything."

"And?"

"Item two, our son, an only child I should add. Supposed to go to college this fall. Now that truly seems a dream. In with the wrong crowd. Pretty much a waste. I don't know him anymore."

"That it?" She dangled the cigarette over the Premier Cable ashtray on the night stand, and with the index finger of her other hand tapped off ash.

"Oh, one more. My sound-sleeping wife. She's either having an affair, which I doubt, or, I suppose, is now interested in things other than sex. It's been months."

"Hmmm. Sounds like you've got too many distractions to do any bungee-less bridge jumping tonight."

"Suicide? Why do you bring that up?"

"I don't know. I was headed for the Broadway Bridge."

He said nothing.

Kim crushed the spent cigarette, motioned for one more.

"Listen, put it this way. I can't jump your bones, I can't have any silliness before I off myself. See what you've done?"

"So, you gonna wait, another night?"

She held the lit cigarette out sideways, eyeing the orange ember, as if mesmerized. He had not openly rejected her. No, it was behind the casual, wealthy front, this tense middle-aged man wanting to talk. Talking, thinking, talking, thinking—just more dust bunnies for her mind. And to jump she needed an empty mind.

"Who knows? Can't hump now. Can't jump now," she said.

"I take it world's not done you any favors."

"I'm no judge on that. Listen, I want to ask you a question."

"Shoot."

"My guess is you've never been unfaithful to your wife. Or, if you have, it was a room-spinning alcoholic haze, right?" His eyes averted hers. "Anyway tonight, you get this idea—pick up some woman, take her to a cheesy motel room," Kim said, wanding the room with her cigarette. "No sex, you stay faithful to the wife you're thinking about leaving, am I right?"

"Possibly. It was just your face back there, something about your eyes gave me this chance."

Kim's head angled over: No way would she indulge him for any replay now. "Say, you could drive me to the bridge."

"Why? You said you won't jump."

"Probably not. But a few weeks, I get my head empty again, I might."

"So you still need to go to the bridge?"

"My personal test. See if I can look, not touch, too."

"I'd feel badly, you went ahead."

"You should feel bad. Messed with my timing." She kicked back the bedding, exposing her legs again, oblivious to any chill.

"That cigarette, what are you doing?"

Kim gripped the cigarette between her thumb and fingers like a surgeon's scalpel, aimed it down and not breathing brought it near her left thigh. Her eyes attended the ember like a mandala. The gods had to admit her intentions were sincere now. She eased it closer so a point of pale skin turned warm orange.

"This won't be a lengthy procedure," she said with a sharp intake of air.

"I were you, I'd think about that more."

She pursed her lips, exhaling softly, as softly as she gave the cigarette ember to her skin. Her thigh stung.

Her eyes blinked and stayed open. A red mark appeared on the hollow of her thigh, the pair of which might have held him fast. She rolled sideways, squelched the cigarette in the ashtray.

"There," she said. "Now the bridge."

"That wasn't because I only wanted talk, was it?"

"No, a souvenir—oh, that smarts—reminds me this close I came and, zigzag, what it was, it left me."

They both got in the car and soon headed west on Broadway. The time at the motel, though brief, allowed the fog to lift and restore sharpness to the neon signs. Block after block with, at that hour, more cars parked than moving, the car lapped up pavement. Then the lighter on the dash popped.

"You know, my last boyfriend smoked Picayune 100s," Kim said, apropos of nothing more than memories—men who sometimes changed her plan, which now, revamped, was unfolding faster, with less consequence than when she left the apartment intent on a simple, final walk through the swirling fog.

"That good or bad," he asked.

"Oh, no morality to it all. Just another coincidence. They happen all the time."

Outside, on the right, a tubular staff towered, held aloft a green, yellow BP sign with halogens that bathed, by the near gas island, a silver Outback and its driver, stock-still, staring ahead. His not driving anywhere, his probably waiting for change reminded Kim of tossing coins with the *I Ching* back at the apartment. The gist of which was crossing a river. An odd sensation between her shoulder blades told her the gods were in on what she was doing. But the hexagram said crossing a river to meet a great man. How could she do that and still jump? She was out of time to decipher that. She had to get on about it, leave the apartment.

But now, seated next to this man, amid the casual wealth of his car, the looming Broadway Bridge in sight, Kim needed no more convincing the gods were for real. She had to go along, help them; she had to nudge this ripe situation.

"Can you wait for me the other end of the bridge?" she said, for was he not, without question, her great man?

"Sure, I can do that. What about where the bicycle crossing turnout is, the other end?"

"Perfect," Kim said.

The approach, this end, to the massive iron-plate drawbridge, however, gave him precious little room to pull over. Before closing the door, she leaned in—said a rushed good-bye—to let her hand once more indulge the soft feel of the leather seat. What might have been his skin.

In its retreat, the fog thickened along the river banks. Beneath the shroud of mist, fog horns crooned, one here, one there. She started the slight incline of the bridge walkway. His car taillights sped forward, broken glimpses between bridge chords, then dissolved in the fog envelope.

She tugged her coat flaps to blunt the wet, cutting chill. A freight train air horn blared from the opposite river bank. The night air was spiced, she guessed, with the off-odor of rehydrated bird droppings that speckled the riveted structure next to her. She was back to those purposeful steps from earlier outside the apartment. Once at the crown of the bridge, she could look, see what she might do.

Below, fog had filled in the river, enticing her with a vaporous blanket into which she might toss herself. She stroked the rough chipped paint of the railing pipe. It was something to remember: Another foggy night might be the time to jump.

That delicate sear on her left thigh wanted to be touched. And oddly, both of her legs felt strong, vibrant as she approached the crown of the bridge. Was it the truck rumbling by, trailing diesel fumes, that sent tremors beneath her feet, that brought her legs alive?

No, she had thought too much about jumping. The lithe musculature of her legs was disobeying her in excitement at this last moment: They would propel her over the railing into the fog bank.

Kim hugged herself, fearful the gods were ready to play one last trick. Tease her, say a great man was on the other side and then at the top of the bridge short-circuit her brain for one fateful misplay.

She slid her tongue on her teeth, found the last essence of tobacco from the cigarettes they shared. Up there, invisible, was he standing beside the open car door, emergency flasher counting off too many seconds? Did he believe she would not jump? Did he think she shammed him with the burn and the vow, that maybe it was some tipoff she would do away with the rest of her body too?

Her legs ached with desire, a desire she gave into.

She ran. Like a gawky teenager, she ran. Her long steps echoed across the wooden planks of the boardwalk and cool air stuck in her throat.

Then winded, droplets on her face, she was at the bridge crown and held the railing with both hands, her body draped to rest there.

She panted. She had not run so hard since she was a teenager. Was this like being a teenager again? Panting after those golden moments when she made out for the first time? Her head hanging over, she sought out the river, saw nothing but steam and realized her legs wanted to run more. She rubbed her hands into her face, tasted the salt of her own tears.

Kim thought again about that lonely man the other end of the bridge and how he might be suffering with every minute, unsure if he would next hear a water splash. She raised her body from the rail and ran.

A passing car honked. Did the guy think a woman odd running, coat flapping, through the fog at three in the morning? She waved. She felt generous. Her great man waited.

Then, the end of the bridge. Her throat tightened as if what her eyes did not see, she could call out from the fog. The turnout for the bicyclists was empty of cars.

There, with the downslope of Broadway left and Lovejoy right from the Y-intersection, she remembered he had said her eyes gave him a chance. She bounced the button for the crossing signal bicyclists used.

Where was he?

She walked a small circle on the sidewalk, waiting.

Why couldn't he stop?

Maybe she would see him again. More probably, the hexagrams would not let it be.

She crossed the road sans bicycle, looked down on Union Train Station. Before the station portico, the outside dome lights of two taxicabs glowed misty. She could take a cab. She walked faster. That would be safer.

"Damn," she said, and it was not the money he skipped paying on her mind. It was simply that now she found she had lost something, something she would have never missed if only she jumped.

FEAR & TREMBLING

You first saw me, Webb Rowalski, palming the steering wheel, my white Buick, when I left the parking caverns of Albina Towers and surfaced in the daylight aboveground. You guessed beside me on the passenger seat I had a business case full of client papers I'd brought from the CPA offices of Ford, Black and Rowalski. So you thought me another dull-beyond-redemption accountant:

Who, his career going nowhere in Bismarck, reluctantly moved out west to Portland, Oregon. Who, twelve workaholic years later, had partnered at a medium-sized regional CPA practice. Who, home-frontwise, shared with a lovely wife and two children (even lovelier) an Irvington bungalow on Northeast 17th. Who, only out of habit, glanced both ways before joining what traffic there was on Lloyd Boulevard. Who, importantly, was old enough for the reading glasses hanging from their keeper cord about his neck.

Yes, you were mostly right to peg me, Webb Rowalski, so: dull but industrious, a middle-aged man driving eastbound with something less than complete attention.

For I was beat down and on my way to church. All of my partners do pro bono and mine—it's tithing in a way—is for the Church of First Christians. I'd worked up the financials from the books. All that stuff beside me on the front seat. That is what I am professionally licensed to do.

What I had was more bad news. Confirmed the empty space in the sanctuary pews was not going away. Suggested offering plates would not be filled. And where we were, cutting back would no longer work. I could only talk with Father Pauley, see how we'd present this to the Board.

I drove, feeling bad, not a lever to pull, not a button to push. What could I do? Shake churchgoers from trees? In these cynical, rude times, it's not popular to be a Christian. People say it's Pollyann-ish: trying to deny dismal reality staring you down.

Well, I, Father Pauley, and others were about to face our moment of truth and no rosy-glasses Pollyanna would set the church right. It would take both faith and persistence. The test of faith was upon us. That was my state of mind driving through the underpass where 16th dips way down past that old railroad right-of-way, completely overgrown with blackberry bushes. Vagrants, hoboes with dogs, lived in there.

I came up the road rise, my knot of worry a-building and then a gut-twister thought: Would we—and we wouldn't be the first to do so—dissolve the church if the money at last dried up? I stopped thinking, for where the road topped off at the cross street, the light was still green. I stepped on it, picked up speed, was going to make that light.

At the intersection, on the curb, was this kid. T-shirt, baggy shorts, everything torn and frayed. Hair stringy, greasy, and blue tattoos his arms over. He was talking on a cell phone, baseball bat in the other hand, looking to cross the street.

And as I say, there was the baseball bat. Due respect to the national pastime, the kid made me go tilt. I'll freely admit that. Never in your life you'd want to see your daughter bring home that sort of guy.

Next he was off the curb, the smart aleck.

He looked at me like I wasn't there. Was I supposed to slam brakes, stop a two-ton car, for him—this idiot who'd have anyone believe he lived out of a Dumpster?

I checked that the light was still green.

Before I'd accommodate him, those tattoos desecrating what body the good Lord gave him, I'd call his bluff. I was legal: green light and in-the-clear.

I floored the throttle. Let him guess what I thought of his nonsense, that prideful need to call attention to himself.

I had the sense a wind gust from the lunging car alone would blow him back.

Eyeball to eyeball, almost, and in a flash—aha—cockiness changed to wide-eyed surprise in his face.

Checked the light: still green. Then this filthy human being gone. Vanished. A thump. Not a hard thump, only a thump. From the back wheel.

In the rearview mirror, nothing. No cars. No pedestrians. Nothing. The other side of the intersection, I again checked the mirror. My solar plexus seized up.

On the pavement, actually sitting up, the grungy kid held a foot with both hands, sort of rocking about like he was in some pain.

Or was he?

I didn't know what to do.

I kept driving, figured this kinda kid was acting out, playing a game. A con. He'd walk up to a car passing by, fall down, pretend to be hurt. Then a shakedown for medical expenses.

Made sense, made me want to speed up, get away from there, except for one thing. That thump from the back wheel. That was his foot. Or was it? No, it had to be the baseball bat. He threw it under the car. Relieved, I kept driving.

Four blocks from the church, a black-and-white police cruiser came my way. He slowed, fired up his roof lights, twinkling red, white, and blue. I didn't want any speeding ticket, so I kept poking along. Stuck to twenty-five, residential zone, then my rearview mirror had the police car turned around, following me. A few blasts from the air horn and I nosed over to the curb, wondering what was up.

The officer explained a white Buick had been positively ID'd by plates in a hit-and-run down the street. With my car being hiked up for towing, I was chauffeured away in the police cruiser to the Northeast Precinct Station. There, the booking officer said I'd be held for questioning and could count on some jail time. I dreaded calling June, my wife. The kid was really hurt. I felt as humiliated as if I'd blown an IRS audit in front of our best client.

I also began to feel the police inquiry might stack the deck against me. In another room, the officer asked me to blow in a black plastic box, a Breathalyzer. "Why don't you test that jaywalker?" I said, trying to hold my ground. I was not at fault.

"We don't know all the facts, Mr. Rowalski. All we have is you leaving the scene of a pedestrian injury."

A Sergeant Kroll came in. He tried to relax me, asking about accounting, my church, how a good guy like me ever got in such a mess.

"So tell me," he said, "you feel that when this young man walked out in the street you stepped on the gas, maybe to scare him? Now, be careful how you answer that. You need to know the young man gave a statement to the officer on the scene. He claims you steered toward him, stepped on the gas, and tried to run him down."

I could barely control myself, not slam the table. What lies. I needed an attorney.

I didn't want to answer the question. Words of mine could be twisted, distorted if I didn't have an attorney with me. So I did a Christian thing, showed I had compassion: "How is he?" I asked.

"How is who?"

"That guy, the one I supposedly ran over, how is he doing?"

"I don't know where he went, and if I knew, I can't say how it's exactly germane to our discussion here." He shook a ballpoint pen like it was a talisman that would wrap everything up. I would sign a confession and Kroll would be on to the next case. "Back to where we were, simple question, You accelerate after seeing that kid?"

I hedged, I hedged. Something about climbing the hill, forgetting to let off the gas, the grungy kid in the street coming at me. But I knew I was on thin ice. A few questions later, I begged off: "I have to talk to an attorney and I don't have one yet."

Next stop was jail. Christian or not, I was there, charged with hit-and-run, being mug shot. And stripped of all clothing, save my BVDs, I put on shock-orange prisoner pajamas. Forget comfort. I had to wear them until June found an attorney to work my release.

Tell you the truth, my preconception about jail was wrong. No zoo bars. Instead, carpeted corridors flanked by cheery pastel walls, a TV glowing inside each small room we passed—a plushness some budget motels might envy.

At 428, my escort, a starched-uniform sheriff's deputy punched the keypad, opened the door. Inside a quizzical-looking Asian man, in his twenties, maybe his thirties, I couldn't tell, sat on a bunk bed and watched me.

The door shut.

The small TV had ten o'clock news. My cellmate said I got the top bunk. He had already taken the bunk on bottom from a guy before me. If I stayed long enough, I could take the bottom bunk.

"So you in for what?" he asked.

I told him.

He was in for car theft. Third time. "Coming here a cost of doing business. I recycle cars. Make owners buy car early, help the economy, no? Cars I pick taken apart expertly, fix other cars damaged. Recycling I do." He looped his hand about and grinned. "Help Mama Earth, no? By the way, my name Eugene."

I introduced myself, didn't mention my line of work. We watched the rest of the news, my troubles thankfully not a feature. Then at eleven the lights went out, the electricity being, my cellmate said, switched off.

Next morning, I was free. Said good-bye to Eugene—turns out his folks were Vietnamese and boat people who renamed him for where they first settled in Oregon. For a moment there, I wanted to meet the rest of Eugene's family, hear their story, but things were moving.

Yep, I left after some quick paperwork for the front desk. Met Mr. Gomez, the attorney June had found and the three of us talked out on the sidewalk. He quickly got to what might happen next: a lawsuit.

At home, I faced two kids. They had to know why I'd spent the night jailbound. "What happened?" Corey, my six-year-old, said.

"It's like this," I said, trying to keep the tone cheery, but not flippant. "I had a car accident yesterday. A young man fell by my car, but I didn't know it at the time and drove away."

"You hit someone?" Emily asked, sucking her thumb under her upstretched T-shirt.

"Worse than that, I ran over his foot."

"Ooh, the foot come off?"

"No, I don't think so. I'm fairly sure he still has his two feet. Anyway, I just wanted you kids to know why I was away."

"Were you really in jail?" Corey asked, balling both his fists.

"Yes, until we got the money to get out."

Having to explain to the kids, and believe me, they asked questions for days, about being in jail was tough. I couldn't keep them from telling their friends about my stayover. They might even brag about it, one up on the other dads, I suppose.

And hearing "Daddy" and "jail" together in my own children's voices started to sap my sense of who I was. I'd worked hard to be responsible—a family man, a partner in the firm—with all that entailed. And then one snippet of time, during which I might as well have sleepwalked for all my awareness, and it changed. I was marched off and locked up, an irresponsible motorist who maimed an innocent bystander. Whatever anchored my belief that I might live a life of goodness was being badly tested.

I went to the church Saturday afternoon, though I should have been at work trying to catch up. Gray, spitting skies outside, the sanctuary was a respite, even with its unheated chill. I felt peaceful, blessed sitting there in the pew, two rows back from the altar.

Although alone in the sanctuary, I felt closer to the Lord. I began to pray the Lord's Prayer. My forearms and clasped hands rested on the hard back of the pew in front.

I prayed slowly, almost a breath to each syllable, to savor the meaning, to let truth bring my spirit life.

Then I prayed for the hapless young man. I prayed for the Lord to forgive me for judging him so severely on mere sight. And I asked forgiveness because I'd been prideful to think, legal niceties aside, I could get away with what I did.

"Webb," I heard a woman's voice behind me. It was June. She knew I was at church to pray. "Webb, Mr. Gomez called."

I stood, walked back to her. Something had rattled her. She moved with such tenseness. "What did he say?" I asked.

"He said the plaintiff's attorney called. That kid is going ahead and filing a lawsuit, wants more than two million dollars."

June's voice hitched when she said that.

"Was he at his office?" I asked.

I had to see Gomez. June again said he was highly recommended, a hotshot only a year or so out of LC Law School. And on the phone with him, I had every confidence he knew his stuff.

First thing Monday, I drove downtown and the idea of a two-million-dollar lawsuit still dazed me. Choices were few. Either settle out-of-court or fight in court, hoping to clear my name too.

It was not an obvious choice and I needed to see Gomez to do anything.

A historical gem of a building in the Skidmore District housed the offices of Gomez & Quinn, Attorneys-at-Law, PC. Inside the front door, a dignified lobby with spiffy ceiling moldings gave a reassuring impression: Others before me had taken the building's one leisurely elevator to the third floor offices of G & Q. Others had, with proper legal counsel, kept their affairs in order. My nerves were settling, but I knew, as a fellow professional, this help didn't come cheap.

The woman at the receptionist desk buzzed Gomez, said I'd arrived, then offered me coffee. I declined, not wanting to encourage my jitters.

Gomez got off the phone. Jet-black hair, wearing stylish Ben Franklin glasses, he still was in his twenties and looked it. Yet when he talked, I took comfort knowing his uniqueness: He graduated tops in his class.

"I'm being sued—why?" I asked once we sat down in his office.

"Webb, the plaintiff's case stands on the leg the kid can't stand on, get my drift?" Gomez leaned forward, his face showing unemotional acceptance that personal injury always would be the lawyer's ticket to billable time.

"The kid was injured *that* badly? They got medical records?"

"Yeah," Gomez said, "doctor's statement here." He snapped a fresh manila folder against his desktop. "Dack Zuster's a real mess, right foot broken in about ten places—bones, ligaments—I wouldn't wager he'll ever walk again normally."

"So what do I do? It wasn't wholly my fault. He jaywalked, practically threw himself under the car."

"His attorneys gonna argue you were careless."

"I had the green light, how do they prove anything?" I realized my voice was edgy, panicky with the idea I might have run out of luck.

"First, the kid's on crutches. That alone has the jury's attention. Then you gotta assume Mr. Zuster on the witness stand will contradict all you say. You say he stepped off the curb, he was clearly out of the crosswalk. He says, he was right between the lines. See my point?"

"But he was going against a red light."

"Hey, and later we could find he's color-blind." His right index finger sprung out. "But now, you see, it's more like a you said, he said stalemate."

"Okay, what's next?" I slumped back in the chair.

"You choose how to respond."

"But if you were in my shoes?"

"Well, I can't see settling with these high numbers. That's a sure loss. I'd go to court, I like our chances. The facts should clear your name and save your financial worth, which, I assume, is not trivial."

"Yeah, I think that's what I want to do." I said, satisfied the harm I caused—though no fault of my own—shouldn't be a reason to frame me.

A month later, we were in a pretrial hearing in a gloomy wood-panelled room at the Multnomah County Courthouse downtown. The lawsuit had been my troubling companion for weeks. A companion I wouldn't shake soon: A young man on crutches had arrived.

Dack, as in Dakota, was smaller than the arrogant maniac looming in my path I remembered. Now, holding himself upright on the crutches was a shriveled version of that monster, a person, in fact, somewhat more my size. And gone were the Dumpster rags; he wore a suit and tie.

Dack swung his frame forward on crutches, trailed by a pair of attorneys, to the plaintiff's table. I realized that, legal matters aside, Dack was suffering. I could only keep praying for his healing. It was what I knew to do. The legal angle was Gomez's.

With everyone seated, the judge, in black robes, gave instructions. I glanced at my life's tormenting presence. In profile, I noted his hair was cut to where conceivably he might apply for a job in my office.

The judge mumbled away. This hearing would disclose relevant facts. Each side would outline a basic approach to spare the trial both surprises and needless delay.

At some point, the judge's voice rose: "Court's recessed until eleven o'clock."

"What does that mean?" I asked Gomez. He was, however, distracted—one of Dack's attorneys beckoned—and he left to huddle across the aisle.

Seconds later, he returned. "Listen, we're breaking for half an hour. Plaintiff attorneys want to talk, no clients present, okay?" Gomez winked like something was afoot.

I sat tight and watched him and Dack's attorneys leave like they were old drinking buddies. I wondered what new surprise would hit. I began praying silently for Dack—abandoned by his legal representatives too—once again mounting his crutches.

Twenty minutes later, Gomez slipped in beside me again, evidently excited that he had good news. "We got an offer. Ten thousand a year for the rest of the plaintiff's working life."

"Ten thousand for life? But he jaywalked."

"The whole problem is you kept driving. They're gonna prove a rational person in your situation would have concluded that he'd run over Mr. Zuster." Gomez paused for effect. "And stopped."

"So what are you saying? I'm really to blame?"

"Yes and no. But the plaintiff's attorneys were dropping big hints that they'd work lots of you left the scene."

I shrugged. I didn't know how any of this was adding up.

"Which means this offer is better than gambling with a jury on two million," Gomez added.

"But you said I could beat this." I didn't like being whipsawed. I wanted Gomez to put up more of a fight.

"Yeah, but that was before this offer: You get off for eight cents on the dollar."

"Ten thousand a year—I don't have that money."

"Wait, remember present value—I've got the exact figure written down here—is only $167,438."

"Okay, where do I get that?"

"You're gonna have to tap your house."

At that moment the judge came back. People rustled about, the bailiff asking them to sit down.

"I have to think about this," I said.

"You've got about fifteen seconds. It's their one-time offer and it's now." Gomez tapped a pencil on the table.

"What if I don't?"

"Simple, they go ahead, take their chances with a jury. Could be worth more than $600,000 for their legal efforts. You want to do that?"

"I'm out of choices, then?"

Gomez smiled the smile of a less than trustworthy dealmaker.

"Okay, there goes our home equity," I said.

Gomez motioned across the way and a few hand gestures and he invisibly moved most of my net worth across the aisle. I feared the next morning I might wake with aching regrets I didn't comprehend just then.

The judge called for order. The lead plaintiff attorney stood and asked to be recognized. "An agreement between the plaintiff and defendant has been reached, your honor."

Then another recess. The judge, Gomez, the two plaintiff attorneys met in judge chambers. Too quickly it seemed, they emerged and the judge announced particulars. Ten thousand dollars a year awarded to the plaintiff until age sixty-seven. An immediate sum payable with a commuted value of $167,438. "So ordered," the judge said, his voice rising. My fate sealed with a gavel rap.

Then something curious happened.

At this time, a fellow easy to overlook caught my eye. This short Vietnamese, who I swear was Eugene the car thief from my stay in jail, had come in the room. I wanted to ask him, Why the shaved head? He was this bald Buddhist monk and walked slowly forward, cat steps, to the knee-high railing behind the seated Dack Zuster.

I had the crazy idea he was going to reach over and touch Dack. But, no, he stood motionless, silent, his hands folded before him. Then Eugene lowered his head, closed his eyes, seemed to slip into meditation. Eerie.

The judge droned on. Documents the plaintiff to make available, when, where.

My attention shifted back to monk Eugene. Now I don't know Asian religions: Eugene the Buddhist monk could also have been Hindu, Shinto, Taoist, Janist, or, for that matter, Christian. I did know, however, he was praying, praying for Dack right there like I'd done. I knew that.

This went on for some time, then Dack pushed the crutches to one side. In fact, put them against the railing by the bald Buddhist, whom Dack smiled at, as if they knew each other.

One attorney whispered in Dack's ear. Dack ignored him, bent down to his foot with the knee-high contraption. Black nylon, black plastic fittings, lots of Velcro.

Then bald Buddhist Eugene opened his eyes. The judge had paused and no one was coughing. Prayerful Eugene looked at Dack and said softly, "You are healed." He bowed toward Dack with a beatific smile.

"Order in the court." The judge struck down the gavel. "Spectators, any talking in this courtroom and the bailiff will remove you."

The healer turned about and left, taking the mysterious inner smile with him.

Dack, the grace of goodness in his face, tugged the Velcro straps of the orthopedic boot and wriggled his foot free.

His attorneys, seemingly confused, nearly fell from their wooden swivel chairs.

"Order in the court. I insist."

"Don't take that off, our whole case depended on your permanent injury."

"I can walk," Dack said. His face glowed like sunrise. "I can't believe it, I am healed." He walked the aisle and kept walking out the courtroom with only the slightest of limps.

My neck, shoulders, and back suddenly flushed with joyful release. That nightmarish moment from five weeks earlier was thrown away. That spot where I crushed Dack's foot underneath the wheel of my car had vanished. I had witnessed a healing of Christ there among us. In the person of Eugene the Buddhist monk. This was my faith at work.

Gomez turned to me with an intensity in his eyes that wanted to burn paper. "We've been had," he spluttered. "No way you ran over his foot. Doctor's letter was fake. And those shyster lawyers."

I thought Gomez had taken leave of his senses. He'd reassured me about the gravity of the lawsuit more than once. "I thought you knew those attorneys, you acted chummy with them."

"Professional courtesy." He waved his hand dismissively. "Never saw a one of them before today. This is ridiculous. I've never, never seen anything as blatant as a healing in the courtroom. Can you believe it?"

I wasn't about to get into discussing faith with Gomez. Still I had be clear on what I was about. "As a matter of fact, yes." If once in my life, I were to see the miraculous happen in my life, I sure wasn't ready to deny it like Gomez. My faith hadn't gone sour on me. I knew that.

"Did you see how that Zuster smiled when he first saw the monk, like they knew each other? It's one big sham. I'm going to move for a dismissal of the award and, with your consent, go ahead and file charges for possible fraud." Gomez took a deep breath as if back on the dry land of legalisms, he had unmasked as ordinary the miracle of minutes before.

I decided to press him. "So you really don't think," I said, "the monk healed Dack?" The abandoned crutches leaned on the railing behind the plaintiff's table. This reminded me of crutches left to hang on the walls of that sanctuary back east where miracles happen quite often.

"No, I don't believe in fairy tales, why do you ask?"

"Then we disagree." Gomez had this look in his face, both

incredulous and empty. I wasn't about to waste my breath. A conspiracy of no less than five people, three of which had to be licensed professionals was far less believable than the miracle we witnessed. "I believe that Dack Zuster was healed. And my faith means I might have to pay the money I owe him."

"So you don't want go ahead and put those crooks behind bars."

"No, I'm sorry. I think we're finished."

And so it was we sat there a few long minutes, Gomez cleaning his spectacles and tight-lipped about our stalemate. The bailiff fetched Dack from the hallway. And I sat there willing to do as Jesus suggested, Pay to Caesar what's his and to God what's his.

Did I learn anything else?

I now drive more carefully, more attentively. I wish, of course, for a another miracle to help my church get on firmer ground financially, but I realize that no one person can do that.

Mainly, I take the road as it comes.

One other thing, two days ago, I was driving down 16th where my car hit Dack. There on the same corner was another young man, dressed not unlike Dack. He held out his thumb, hitchhiking. I rolled the window down, asked if he wanted a ride. He said he'd been waiting more than half an hour and got in.

Part of the old me would have wanted to ask if he'd received the Lord Jesus into his heart. But I knew it was enough to simply share what I had with this young man and let it be.

We drove on through intersections and I felt as if my heart was, for one of the few times in my life, beginning to open. I was taking it in. Caring for others, this hitchhiker beside me. I was happy only because I finally knew I had much to give others, even complete strangers and I was no longer afraid. That was it, I was no longer filled with, as Paul would say, fear and trembling. I could have at that moment died straight away and known I was saved. Completely saved.

We drove on and the hitchhiker, as if in that intimate space of the car unknowingly shared my revery of reverence, said, "You saved me."

MARBLES ON THE LOOSE

In chuffing motions high and wide, the young woman rubbed a chalkboard eraser through the examples of Palmer penmanship for the letters *s* and *t*. She had run out of time because of the interruption. The special way to make a small *t* at the end of a word would have to wait for next class, she had told students as they streamed out for recess.

From beyond the empty desks came the sound of glass clicks. She turned and looked at a fat boy kneeling on the floor beside a bulging Gold Medal Flour sack.

"I be done."

He rose, shifted his weight from one foot to the other, and cast a final, searching glance downward. His brow, freckled darkly, furrowed.

"I'm sure, Benno, you got them all."

"Yes, Miss Arguello. If I can get anybody to play, I win more. I *Mister* Marbles King."

"I *am* Mister Marbles King, Benno."

"Yes'm."

Benno left, tennis shoes thumping, squealing over the waxed corridor. The marbles sack swung by its drawstring. He tramped down the stairs, intent on the playground, when girls from class—Shonda, Tori, and Annrae—stopped talking and to a one beamed at him.

"Your marble bag not looking too heavy," said Tori.

Shonda asked if he missed any. Annrae's eyes cut from Shonda to Benno, her mouth open like she wanted to say something.

"Not none," he said.

"I saw Jared pick up some by his desk," said Annrae.

"Oh, you be jiving me." Benno walked sideways past the three, not missing a step.

"Bag look smaller," Shonda yelled after him. He pushed open the metal door with its small, sunlit wire-mesh window and went outside.

A riot of kids played four-square, hopscotch, tether ball, kickball in the far corner, and game after game of marbles, where guys hunched over white circles chalked out on the black asphalt.

Benno waggled the taut drawstring, then set the marbles sack down and crossed his arms, as proud a figure as Michael Jordan. Unlike Michael, he had no takers in his game. These guys wouldn't make room. They'd point to the sack, ask what he wanted with more marbles.

Benno wondered when he'd ever play marbles again. Below a forehead of Jheri curls, his dark eyes squinted. He checked off all the good players who refused to play. It was everyone, including nappy-head Jared in the nearest game. Annrae's words came back. That sneaky thief. He uncrossed his arms, picked up the marbles, and walked.

"Let me in this game, man," he said.

"You late out the gate, spilling marbles."

How could Jared be second-best marbles player at Irvington, he always having excuses not to play? "Jared, let me in, I forget you pick up my marbles back there."

"Who said that?"

"Someone. A girl."

"What you see?"

"Am I going to play or not?" Benno said. His fingers itched to shoot marbles.

"No, find your own game."

"What say I don't play for keepsies?"

Jared ignored him.

Pressure built in his chest. He trudged to another game. If he was forced to spectate, it would be away from someone for whom he was half ready to bust their lip.

Benno parked his marbles and stood next to E.C., the perpetual, unpopular loser in school. Skinny as a green bean, E.C. had a marbles bag filled probably with fifty cents worth of new cat's-eyes bought that week.

E.C. tilted his head back and said, "Want to play? Not easy get in a game." Benno wanted to laugh. Poor E.C. Poor Benno. They were both desperate, any game was better than none.

Benno knew an empty marbles circle by the school building, under the fire escape from the second floor. He took out a piece of chalk and touched up the lines.

"What game we play?" said E.C.

"Your choice," said Benno.

"Oh, whatever you guys be playing most is okay."

"Then it's potsie. We both put in five." E.C. counted out five marbles from the pathetic marbles bag. "Let's not bother lagging," Benno said. "You go ahead, shoot first." Benno dropped the ten marbles in the middle of the circle. Out of his pants pocket came his favorite shooter, an aggie he discovered in a neighborhood vacant lot years ago where for weeks and weeks the Kuwaiti army he'd joined dug trenches in a game of Desert Storm. Ugly, but the pitted aggie felt like sandpaper and could he ever give it spin.

On his first try, E.C. dribbled out, missed it all. He shot like a girl.

"Slippsie," Benno yelled as he got down next to E.C. to show him how cocking his thumb would give some power, some control. Any hope for a little competition was gone. His opponent had just shelled out five marbles for Benno's target practice. E.C. missed again. Ouch.

Settling on his knees, he got ready to shoot, became still and pensive as a stone sculpture. Only his eyes darted about, as if catching the marbles in motion from different shot possibilities. Might as well stretch out the game; it would be over soon enough.

He knocked out five in a row and each time the aggie stuck at the point of impact, a spinning blur. When the fifth rolled out, Benno quit staring at the marbles and gave E.C. a quick look.

E.C. still grinned like he was enjoying the game. Benno decided the guy needed at least one more turn shooting. He set up for a combination shot, a really hard one.

Two marbles flew out. Benno chuckled at his failure to lose his turn. He aimed at one of the three marbles left and shot the aggie flat, without spin, and the cat's-eye was his. The aggie also rolled out. Great. E.C. can shoot again.

E.C. missed again.

Benno didn't like it. After a whole week of not playing anybody, he ends up having a guy practically give him marbles. And why was E.C. so happy about losing? Was it the thing about being lonely, especially lunchtime in the cafeteria? That had to be the worst. Benno remembered E.C. sitting at a cafeteria table in back. Alone, sticking to his slicing off bites of steamy meatloaf and eating mushy spinach.

Benno stopped thinking and knocked out the rest.

"Man, I wish I play like that," E.C. said. "Hurry, let's play another before recess is over."

Benno didn't know what to think. Was E.C. ready to lose five more? Words caught in Benno's throat. He was done taking this guy's marbles and nobody else would play him.

Benno crouched beside the bulging marbles sack planted on the ground. Yanked open its mouth. Miss Arguello would have nothing to say about this. The top marbles clicked at his touch. Yellow, red, blue wisps of color in the cat's-eyes wanted to be rolling. No one had ever done this.

He grabbed marbles like they were free jelly beans, spilling some, then rose back up. E.C.'s face seemed lost at what was happening. Sun-bright clouds floated in the blue above and that's where his right arm catapulted dozens of marbles in a high arc. Sunlight glittered off the glass missiles. Then they crashed and ricocheted on the asphalt. "Free marbles," Benno shouted.

The sound of skipping marbles was followed by the scuffling of kids. He reached down, scooped another handful of marbles. "Get out there." He waved E.C. back.

E.C.'s face smiled all over. "You badder than I thought, Benno."

As if he needed to know where to aim, the voices came at him: "Over here, Benno. Benno, us too. Yea, Benno." He reached back and slung skyward his gift. The voices retreated, guessing correctly that he was going for distance. Marbles rained down and bounced like hail. Guys were colliding and Benno drew a deep breath. It was like Halloween treats, Christmas presents, and an Easter egg hunt rolled into one. The fighting over marbles was both crazy and happy. He loved it.

The voices: "More, throw more, please. Throw some over here. Benno, you style, man."

The voices and another reach in the marbles sack. Then the flinging skyward one handful of marbles.

The voices, more marbles skipping through the scurrying feet. And scooping out more marbles and the sound of those voices wanting him not to stop.

Over and over, the glassy spheres catapulted from Marbles King's arm until the voices and the tossing to the sky could not go on. His fingers at last felt hard asphalt under the marbles sack, flopped over like a torn balloon. Benno clutched the sack and shook the rest of the marbles out. He kicked a few.

"You got them all." He waved the empty sack like a flag.

Benno stood up straight and checked it all out. Guys pig piled on each other for the last marbles. Even E.C. mixed it up. Benno laughed at E.C. and another guy both reaching under the chain-link fence for some marbles off the playground. And Jared ran about greedy as the rest of them. Jared was coming around. He knew who was Mister Marbles King and next thing he'd be thanking Benno personally. Benno couldn't believe it. This was the best thing he'd ever done in his life.

When the scuffling was over and the last cat's-eye pocketed, Jared swaggered up. He held his marbles sack to his chest, almost as if to point out that he had the most marbles. "Benno, you're dumb. You know that."

Benno's hands felt heavy, almost like a fight coming on.

"You ought to take that empty bag, put it over your head," Jared said as if he hadn't been out there running after marbles.

Benno's teeth clamped together. He wanted to bite off, spit out Jared's little nappy head. He tore Jared's sack away, loosened the drawstring, gave it a shaking until all the marbles were out, rolling. Then he kicked at what he could, splattering marbles every which way. "More free marbles," he yelled.

"You cocksucker," Jared said. He grabbed his marbles sack. He turned to the others, "Bring them here, they're mine."

Benno laughed. He twirled his own empty marbles sack about his head.

"You going to pay for this. You are," Jared said.

The next day, Benno was a hero. Everyone who rushed up to him had the ebullience of a winner with marbles to spare. They said Benno really fixed Jared, who only played guys much worse than he, who deserved what he got. Now Jared was cleaned out, they said, laughing.

They pleaded with him to play. But Benno would not take the marbles guys offered. He wanted to soak up being a philanthropist and watch the guys, even E.C., shoot marbles.

Recess after recess, he'd go from game to game, making expert comments, in a low voice, about who was winning and why. He was the perfect spectator and he relished how everyone kept beaming at him. They kept grabbing at his arm to play.

Not that he didn't want to play again ever. Now and then when his shooter thumb got itchy, he'd reach in his pocket for his last marble. He'd pinch his trusty aggie and rub his thumb back and forth over its pitted surface, then put it back in his pocket. He knew he could beat any of them, but for now being popular was what he wanted.

After all, that was how come he threw out the marbles. One person, though, wasn't rushing over to get Benno in a game. Jared. He had also quit playing marbles. Almost like he wanted everyone to know he held his grudge dear.

So dear that one morning, on the way to school, Benno got some dirty looks from Jared and two other guys leaning against a fence. They smoked cigarettes, something they must not have wanted their parents or teachers to know, but something they were not hiding from every other kid in school.

Jared stubbed out his cigarette on the fence and strolled out on the sidewalk. So did his two icy-eyed friends. They acted like hard guys, blocking Benno's way.

"You owe for marbles, where's your lunch money? Where's your seventy-five cent?" Jared said.

"You jive turkey. I be shivering and quivering so bad."

Jared flung his hand out, palm up. "Hand it over."

"Man, your marbles worth nothing. Here." Benno fished three quarters from his pocket and chunked them at Jared's feet.

"This only one day's payment, blood." Jared stood tight with his buddies, forcing Benno to walk around them, off the curb. Next time, Benno knew, was fight-time.

That afternoon, once school let out, Benno headed for church. He needed to go to confession.

In the booth, he fidgeted on the skinny wooden seat, not sure what to say first. He couldn't sit speechless too long. The priest might come around, checking if he was okay. "Father, I'm in trouble bad," he said softly.

"What trouble, my son?" It was the familiar, optimistic voice of Father Pauley. He could be trusted with anything. Had client privileges, like on TV.

"I dumped out Jared's marbles and kicked them all over the playground."

"You do want to replace them, don't you?"

"Should I? When I did that, he be laughing at me, said I was stupid after I threw away all my marbles."

"What? You're saying you don't have marbles to give Jared?" Father Pauley always started with lots of questions.

"Yeah and what's more, he and his friends shaking me down for my lunch money." His shoulders sagged.

"Well, that's extortion—does your school principal know about this?"

"No. I wanted to see what you'd say, what you'd say about me throwing away his marbles." He stared at the cloth-covered opening inside the booth, waiting for the disembodied voice from the other side. What could Father Pauley say? Both he and Jared were in the wrong.

"You're impulsive, son, but young; you have much to learn. I'm sure God forgives you. He knows you want to do the right thing."

"Me give Jared lunch money?"

"No, no, absolutely not. Next time you see him, tell Jared you'll give back all his marbles. Just make sure he understands you'll need some time to buy them."

"Or win them back." Benno pressed his palms down on his thighs.

"Yes. And as for the lunch money, be sure and walk with another friend, someone to be your witness. I bet Jared won't be so bold if you're not alone."

Benno pushed up off the wooden bench and said thanks. He didn't have to say one Hail Mary. The worst was over.

Benno wasn't sure about Father Pauley's advice to walk with a friend, but he found another way home, one that didn't include the usual swing by QwikBuy for candy. And if Jared and his buddies spent too much time waiting for him the next street over, that was okay.

But that didn't keep Jared away at school. One recess Benno was crossing the playground, kids were shouting and running, and Jared called out to him, "Where you hiding yourself after school, blood?"

Benno felt power from his shooter thumb all the way up to his punch-'em, drop-'em biceps. That beady-head Jared came closer, so Benno shot back, "Still want those marbles?"

"That skinny bag, you never pay back. I need money."

"No money, you get them end of month," Benno said, firm like Father Pauley in confession, who told him what was right to do.

Jared's shifty eyes froze up like, What was Benno saying? "You owe all of them, all them two hundred marbles."

Benno hitched up his sagging pants, rubbed his hands together like the matter was done. He had games to play, marbles to win. "You come by my place end of month, I'll take care of you," he said like he'd dismissed some runt-sized bro.

Jared, empty-faced, had no comeback.

Every recess, Benno was at it. Winning a few marbles here, there. Working with his revived popularity and not playing anybody more than twice a day. Just moving around from game to game, so the word wouldn't spread too fast that the old killer form was back.

He'd play anybody, even E.C., whom he hated to take marbles from, the guy was such a dufus player. But E.C. didn't seem to mind, he was glad to have a game.

The retarded players that were difficult were like that runny-mouth Deanerio. Once, behind him, Benno *heard* Deanerio playing a game with E.C. and he asked to get in.

Deanerio said he'd play if he and E.C. put in four each and Benno put in eight.

"Oh, man, Deanerio, you forget Benno threw out his marbles?" E.C. said. "What you thinking?"

"His handicap, he better than us. He gotta put in more."

Deanerio would like to become a fine lawyer: slow game and plenty of argument. Benno wasn't about to talk away any more recess. He put in the marbles, eight.

E.C. won the lag from Deanerio—Benno shooting third—another concession to legal man. E.C. fumbled out with an old lady shot and hardly disturbed the bunched-up marbles.

Deanerio, for all the jive, shot one marble out. Next, shot, he didn't stick the shooter, lost the turn.

Benno hunched over, calculating the easy shot, the leave, the next shot. He cocked his thumb till it blanched tan and his eyes raked to the target cat's-eye and *clack*, the aggie took it out. He moved in the circle. *Clack*, three inches away, the second cat's-eye. The aggie spun up a blur. *Clack*, a third cat's-eye. *Clack. Clack. Clack. Clack.* Benno eventually took them all.

"Another game?" Benno asked. He dropped the winnings in the open mouth of his flour sack.

"The way you play, you gotta put in more, put in sixteen, we put in four. That's your new handicap." Beating Deanerio had a big price, like marbles were only the excuse to argue.

E.C., always agreeable, smiled.

"What if I put in four," Benno asked, "E.C. put in four, you put in zero?" With that remark, Benno knew Deanerio joined Jared on the new list of guys that would refuse to play. His stomach suddenly felt hollow at the idea that he could have everyone quit playing on him before he'd won enough marbles.

That night, Benno watched his mom wash dishes with a soapy rag. She had her hair up, she was perspiring, she looked slimmer than usual wearing that stained and frayed apron. He ate oatmeal raisin cookies, his favorite, and drank milk.

"Benno, why you so hungry? You ate dinner only two hours ago."

"I be having some dessert, a nightcap before bed."

"What a growing boy you are. I just wish more of you would grow up than out."

The reminders about his weight were so tiresome. He toyed with the empty milk carton, held it up. "Mom, you mash these, be recycling, don't you?"

"Why you ask?"

"I just wonder if I can have them for keeping stuff."

"You wash it first, hear."

A guy Benno did like to play was Cleveland. Cleveland was good. Quiet, all concentration. A lot like Benno's style.

They'd stopped by a chalk circle the top of the playground, next to the brick school building, well away from screeching hopscotchers. Once his growth spurt started, Cleveland got to be a long, tall hoopster. Benno was afraid he'd quit marbles altogether, make basketball his main game.

"You like potsie, seven in each?" Benno asked his towering companion.

"Potsie's okay, but I rather play honeypotsie. You cool on that?"

"Honeypotsie? Whoa!" Benno didn't know. Chancy game.

Cleveland tossed his marbles bag between his two palms, sized like pancakes.

Benno had to take it or leave it. Cleveland looked elsewhere, moved his head with a b-ball fake, like he was peeping another game across the way. The game was all or nothing. Knock out the honeypot marble and everything else was his. Benno could use seven quick marbles. He held out a black purie. "For the honeypot, we use this." With one hand, Cleveland wrapped his long fingers around the marbles bag and with the other, counted out the seven marbles they were each in for.

Cleveland won the lag and let Benno go first. To dislodge the honeypot, center of the bunch, on the first shot was almost impossible. Benno knelt, fired his aggie, slightly off to the right. Three marbles popped loose.

Cleveland's turn. Again, like Benno, he broke a few away from the bunch.

Benno scooted to the other side. Attack the marbles from there. It did no good to hit the honeypot, unless it could roll out. He aimed once more off center, his aggie rifling across the asphalt and slamming the bunched marbles. The aggie stuck, spun furiously in place. Three more marbles scattered.

Cleveland concentrated, like thought energies would move marbles, give him an opening. Hopeless. On all sides, the black purie was blocked. Cleveland squatted, his fist just outside the chalk line, pitted shooter snug against his thumb. Benno laser-eyed the thumb, tried giving it a jinx. A flick and out shot the missile, blasting the marble in front of the honeypot. Almost quicker than Benno could follow, the black purie popped up like a Fourth of July rocket. He held his breath.

The black purie came down and rolled. Benno felt like someone had personally stuck a cold stiletto knife in his belly. He'd never seen this happen before. The black purie rolled across the chalk line, out and game over. He was dead, then he looked around.

That nappyhead Jared had seen the whole thing, gave Benno a mocking eye. "You ain't about nothing." Benno looked away. Cleveland was quietly gathering all he'd won. "That bag of yours, it too skinny," Jared said, now louder.

Benno glowered back at Jared. "What I tell you, you get paid end of the month." He had just lost seven marbles and didn't have the energy to bust that flicted grin off Jared's face.

"You lose bad here, I worry."

Benno said nothing. Turned away and walked.

That Jared was pure pest. A chigger bug that won't let off biting your arm. Benno couldn't shake him. One way or the other, he'd pay him back. He'd do just that. Do what Father Pauley said was right.

If Jared wasn't enough of a bother, Benno was also getting irked by the sight of Theron, who'd taken to bragging on himself, toting around his fat marbles sack, claiming to be the best. Benno wanted to take him out, get some marbles to boot.

One day Benno asked him, "You want to play the best, Mr. Big Bag?"

Theron's caramel eyes glanced up at his, then down. "Man, I busy with this game." Zeke, who always shot hard and wild, knelt at the circle too.

"You about finished."

Theron ignored him.

"You selective, you don't go bragging near me. You know you play me, you choke."

Theron picked off a marble, a shot sweet as biting a gumball. The shooter spun, setting up a cripple shot, inches away. Bang, the game was done.

"You sure you can afford to lose five marbles?" Theron asked, the caramel eyes checking out Benno's slack bag of hard-won marbles. He nodded at Zeke like he'd agree Benno was yesterday's oatmeal.

"I'm in for five," Benno said, flicking his shooter thumb over and over like some Zippo lighter. He stood ready to beat the black off that Theron.

Theron squatted, bunching up the ten marbles, middle of the ring. They lagged, Benno lost, and Theron shot first. The shooter flew at the target, knocking one marble loose for a roll to the feet of Zeke. The shooter stuck for a choice of good shots.

Bam. Second marble out. Benno studied the marbles hard. He needed his turn. This Mr. Big Bag was no jive turkey. Theron was good, shot like a young Benno.

The next shot was tricky. Wham, the marble went out, so did Theron's shooter.

Benno got busy. His turn and he was going to have to blast and hope for the best. A hard shot. Anything less wasn't going to break a marble loose.

He closed his eyes, imagining a miracle shot, every last marble rolling out simultaneously. His eyes open, calm, he read the three feet of asphalt out to the marble bunch. He put his left fist under his right fist for an air shot. The thumb tightened up behind the aggie until his thumb bones would pop, then without realizing it, the aggie shot out like a bomb—*clickety-clickety-clickety*—the marbles exploded all over. Two went for the chalk lines.

The trusty aggie spun in the damage. Benno exhaled big relief. He was even with one shot.

Bang. Bang. Bang. Three shots, three marbles. Fourth shot, Benno's shooter went out too.

He studied caramel eyes for signs of fear. Benno could not lose, only tie with five marbles now.

Theron set up for the three remaining cat's-eyes. His shooter skipped out, took a bad bounce, missed everything. Benno bit his tongue. A young Benno would have made the same mistake, not going for the air shot.

Benno felt like he was closing in for the kill. He pinched his ear lobe and cooly eyed Theron's fat sack. Mr. Big Bag, ha-ha, he gonna have a hard fall. He knew.

He steadied down at the chalk line. Another air shot. Like a rifleman, he picked one cat's-eye off, sent it scuttling out of the ring. The shooter stuck near the other two. Bang. Bang. Game over.

"Another game?" Benno asked.

"No, I gotta play Zeke, win some marbles back."

Zeke playacted horrified, palms up, fingers spread.

"Anyone else?" Benno said to the crowd of fool grinners who'd joined Zeke on the sidelines.

Benno had no takers. Killer Benno. He was going to lose his popularity again. "You not being afraid to play me. Check this." He rattled the sack, the few handfuls of marbles at bottom stretching the fabric of the bag that held mostly air.

"Yeah, man, you having one big sack before long, way you thrashed Theron. He's good," that punk Warren said.

"Yeah, big sack, I throw them all away again, maybe." Benno shook his head. These fools don't know what marbles about. Win, lose, it was all playtime. Anybody ever actually eat marbles? He chuckled.

Amid the commotion, Jared showed his face.

"Okay, blood, tomorrow end of month. You owe," Jared said. His sweaty, beady head had angry eyes.

"You get the marbles, chill," Benno said, letting his marbles sack twist lazily on its drawstrings.

"Two hundred. Two hundred marbles. You ain't got that in that bag."

"You get 'em, don't be sweating no BB's."

"Sure, yo mama buy you them marbles, or you in bad business."

"Like what?" Benno asked, ready to laugh at the eyes half filled with anger, half filled with fear.

"Like I'm suspended out of school, you be laying in hospital bed," Jared snapped.

"You get 'em tomorrow."

"Like when, where?"

"We go my place after school." Benno shrugged his indifference. Jared could believe him or not.

Next day, they stood in Benno's room where a poster of Michael Jordan covered most of a wall. "Blood, why you be keeping all these milk cartons like that?" Jared shot a finger at five milk cartons that sat along the wall below the poster.

"I keep track how I'm doing, hundred marbles in each," Benno said, a smile sneaking across his face, sassy as his jerry curls.

"Those filled with marbles?" Jared said, his eyes wider. "What your flour sack doing? You supposed to show them marbles."

"New 'tude. I'm Mr. Humbles." Benno tugged up his pants, didn't bother with the shirt, half out.

"Uh, huh. What's with you? Ain't you no pride about winning?"

"No, it's complex situation. I start setting aside some to pay you back, then I see guys they thinking I'm losing 'cause my bag don't get no bigger."

"Like Theron." Jared had gone and busted loose his first smile.

"Yeah, I beat him bad, but guys still be feeling sorry for me 'cause I don't carry all them marbles."

"And they no mind you win now?"

"I even be staying popular," Benno said.

"Sounds me like you be steady hustling everybody, only getting better at it." What had come over Jared? He almost looked like he could be a friend.

"Like I say, call me Mr. Humbles. I ain't be living *large* no more."

Secrets had to be secrets, Benno added. He clumped over to the all-Mr.-Air-Jordan wall, knelt and rattled a milk carton in each hand, told Jared he'd be best keeping most of them at home.

THE PRESIDENT, HE SLEPT HERE

Blue sky above, the whitest snow—plum blossoms—bedded a stretch of Klickitat Street. A solitary man, Pliny, cane in hand, companion radio to his ear, suggested a college wrestler from the lighter weight classes—his spine arched forward—warily making his way. But really, Pliny was vintage. Two years ago in 1997, he had topped, as they say, the century mark.

    The crablike steps halted. Porkpie hat sheltering his bald head, khaki windbreaker, a Stewart tartan Pendleton shirt, some denim dungarees, Pliny leaned on the cane as if by a thought arrested. Here, enjoying the wayward breezes of March 20, 1999, and out walking to shake up his hundred-two-year-old bones, he saw his tombstone, what might be written there.

    That is, if he finished out the year. On January 1, 2000, a new century would begin, at least the way he counted. And if he was still standing New Year's Day next, he could lay claim to having lived in three centuries because that tombstone would say, 1897—20XX. Those X's for whenever his Maker punched his ticket to fly free through the cosmos.

    The feet in red socks and dingy tennis shoes, the cane, again inched forward. He liked this sidewalk: no toe-stubbers catching him off guard. He didn't know when, where he'd leave, so he tried to take the best from every day. Didn't skip his walk for rain. Only ice kept him inside. As he told his caregiver, Maud, he just didn't feel right if his bones missed a good daily shaking.

And he could've added, if he didn't get angry listening to talk radio.

He thumb-rolled the volume, pressed the radio to his ear.

"And our guest today, Dr. Jonathan Strickland, is talking about the new medical marijuana law, which has only been in effect a few weeks—so give us a call."

Those damn Baby Boomers. They get sick, gotta smoke that locoweed. And they get sick and old, they throw in the towel, ask doctors to drug them dead.

Pliny clicked the radio off.

Death with dignity, they call it. What rubbish. I'd never make it this far thinking like that. You ask me, they're yellow—got no more backbone than a slug.

Ahead, small kids played baseball cross-street. He pinched the old leather case on the transistor radio. Where was the world going? He'd tune the Sony to KGUF and in minutes some asinine topic like this medical marijuana. He wanted to find and wrestle all those airwave crazies to the ground, make them admit they were wrong. And now he was mad, could spit blood, but he felt good.

One kid swung the bat, *kerplopped* the green, fuzzy tennis ball, and ran.

"Foul ball. Strike two. You come back."

"No way. That was in."

"Are you crazy, that bounced behind first base, I saw it."

Pliny squinted. Those arguing youngsters, damn Baby Boomers for parents. What did they have for a future?

Environment a shambles, the politicians back East, greedy corporations throwing people out of work, when were things ever this bad? Pliny's one wish, when his time came, was to leave Earth on some kind of high note. Say, like that time the President stayed overnight right here in Irvington. But the current mess—no, messes—he might not outlive.

A kid yelled, "Time out!" Several kids said dutiful hi's. Pliny paced his way across the street and from their courtesy, gave the kids a second chance to turn out okay and set things right. But they still needed more the real life to toughen them up, not that playing video games.

An empty block before him, Pliny clicked the radio on, brought it to his ear.

"Some medical conditions pot helps."

Ha! Those kids better watch out for ol' Grandma, her secondhand smoke, she gets one of those permits to self-medicate. It's a crazy world. Say, maybe I can't leave too soon.

Pliny listened, crab-stepping, negotiating sidewalk squares, radio first pressed to his ear, then held away, then back to his ear.

Brrrmmmmm. Overhead, a commuter plane readied for a landing at the airport by the Columbia River, the pilot taking the high-wing turboprop, sun glinting off its wings, in for a slow descent.

Yes, like that pilot, he just tried to get through life the best he could—clean living, hoping his earthly journey ended with a smooth landing.

He turned off the radio. Enough of that angry tonic.

Suddenly, from nowhere and now beside him in an outsized blue nylon parka this young black kid joined Pliny's deliberate steps.

"Mister, you old be walkin' out by yourself, how old you be?" The kid's face was sullen, but the cheery voice seemed to yearn for some fun.

"What's that? I know you?" How direct this younger generation was: this kid, a complete stranger, asking him his age. "I'm Pliny. What's your name?"

"Me? Oh, my name Jared. So how old, Mr. Pliny, you be?"

"One hundred two."

Jared jumped out in front of Pliny on the sidewalk, backstepping, shifty eyes wide open. "Whoa, you that old? Better watch your back. You need protection bad."

"Protection?" Pliny furrowed his brow. What can this skinny black kid possibly be talking about, he's shorter than I.

"Check this out. I got it new, a stiletto." Jared fished from the parka pocket a long knife, eight inches, at least. The bolsters, black plastic with an intricate inlaid metal design. He pushed a knobbed lever at one end and out flipped the spring-loaded blade.

Pliny gasped and, resting on his cane, stood stock-still. That blade, razor-sharp, seemed long enough to go in his chest and out the back. The black kid waggling the knife. Pliny's hand, frozen to the crook of the cane, lifted. Cane forward. Foot forward. He had to walk, had to say something.

"Stiletto, that sounds Italian," he said, with small satisfaction his gruff tone hid his shock at the weapon Jared freely displayed.

"Italian. Oh, yeah." Jared turned, walked forward. "The Godfather he be steady packin' one these. You feel safer already, huh, Mr. Pliny?" Then, without comment, Jared folded the knife blade back and slipped it in the pocket of his baggy parka.

Relieved, the weapon out of sight, Pliny felt he could speak his mind. Kids, senseless violence. "You ever think, someone saw you carrying that big knife, they'd think it's okay to knife you first?" He raised his cane tip off the ground, pointed it at Jared.

"Man, out here it's eye for eye like the Bible done said. I got myself to protect."

"Live by the sword, die by the sword," Pliny said loudly.

His companion grinned. "Hey, Mr. Pliny, I gotta book." He glanced away. "My crew—the Thirteenth Street Slitters—we be meeting over at Alameda School, right now." And those quick words out, Jared strided across the street, up 22nd.

Pliny's bones ached with great fear for the young black.

He couldn't start thinking where that life would go and leaned on his cane, thumb-clicked the radio, and slow walk underway, took in another earful.

"And besides they outlawed Freon—when?—right after the patent expired."

Criminy, not another conspiracy nut. People like her are a big waste of time, terrible waste, but I can't listen to anything else. They stopped playing my music so long ago. Oh, Bix Beiderbecke, he was something.

"Now what's your point?"

"No scientist, no responsible scientist has proved . . ."

Wait, what's this? Cane out of my hand. Cane on the sidewalk tripping me. Legs buckling. What? Oh, hard concrete. Back of my hand hurting, pinned on the cane.

Grassy smell.

Funny leg. Not moving.

Warm taste. Wet warm running down chin.

A little rest, then getting up.

"It's okay, stay here," the comforting voice says from nowhere.

Black everywhere.

Oh, crazy leg. Twitching and lame.

Slowly, slowly, stopping the world.

So quiet. Deaf and warm taste. Lost words. Forgotten sound.

Painful throbbing hand.

"And look at all the good Jimmy Carter is doing," the voice says from far away, from nowhere, from anywhere.

Nothing here. Nothing.

I'm up again, not even a cane. Where am I? It's 16th below Brazee, a huge crowd, the street blocked off. Here with my dear Sophie behind a wrought-iron fence 'round the front yard this big old Dutch Colonial, white with dark green shutters. I point at that door, all its polished brass, and tell Sophie, "The President, he slept here last night. He's inside right now."

She turns, her hair in a tight, fussy bun. "And you, of all people, get to meet Jimmy Carter!"

Secret Service—tall, muscular guys—everywhere and giving this crowd a real lookover.

Kids, parents, they're all chattering away; they want Jimmy Carter to finish his Presidential eggs and bacon; they can't keep their eyes off that front door, the microphone booms and TV cameramen, left and right. Everyone knows that that's the door.

"Ladies and gentlemen, members of the press." The guy speaking with the Southern accent, the short blond hair, he glances our way and I realize it's Jody Powell, the President's press secretary who's always on TV, except, of course, here, no TV studio, just tall trees overhead and crows cawing away.

"Pliny, I've been looking all over for you." Mrs. Reyes—I haven't been able to find her—pulls on my arm. "Hurry up, we're supposed to be over there."

We squeeze past the front gate—unbelievable, I'm leaving the crowd, even Sophie, because Mrs. Reyes has this ID.

Sudden cheers and the front door opens.

Jimmy Carter is shorter than I thought. Oh, five-seven, five-eight, but an upright posture from the military. Got on a dark suit and tie; he's probably meeting the locals down at City Hall for lunch; though for us, a cardigan and chinos would have been fine.

He's at the microphone and my neck feels prickly in back. Less than twenty feet away it's *us* he's talking about: the turnaround, people moving back to the inner city, learning lessons for elsewhere.

It's a quick speech and Jody Powell steps up and says with the tight scheduling, questions must wait until the noontime briefing downtown.

The President comes this way with Powell. Some woman stops him, talks with him. Now, he's right here, grinning recognition like he knows who we are.

"Mr. President," Mrs. Reyes says, "I'd like to introduce several of the Irvington Neighborhood Association's real doers." We all mumble, "Pleased to meet you." She says a little about me.

"So you're a real spark plug for good work, getting all those trees planted," the President says. The clear gray eyes pay attention to no one but me. I know I must say something. The President is waiting. The minicams are rolling. My mouth wants to say words, but the more I try, the blanker my mind seems.

I smile so he knows I heard him. He flashes the toothsome smile and before it fades, I blurt out, "Mostly maple, yes, that's what we planted, we planted mostly maple."

I can't believe what I said. Like some green eyeshade accountant, I start an inventory for the President of the United States about what we stuck in the ground?

But remarkably, it's exactly right saying this. "Maples, oh, fine choice," Carter says. "They're a high-quality, strong tree. And they'll last long after"—the dimple between his eyebrows moves—"we've all gone to our Maker."

"I keep a watch on my trees, sir." I am aware he's from the South, where the ma'am's and sir's are habit. "I'm retired, eighty-one this year, so I have time to do what good I can. Otherwise, I suppose I'd just be living longer to grow wronger."

The President grins and puts his hand to my shoulder. "Eighty-one? You don't know how heartened it makes me feel that people like you are volunteering to beautify your neighborhood."

"Oh, it's nothing."

"Your teamwork is just fine, I'll be telling my mother, Miss Lillian, about the cooperative spirit out here in Oregon the next time I see her."

I want to warn Jimmy about that hostage thing coming up, but it's too late. Smiling eyes, toothy grin, all his attention's with Connie Brennemann next to me; she got the Neighborhood Watch program going. I'd just spoil the occasion. And who else understands this Iran thing?

He sidesteps away, greeting others, then there's a limousine from somewhere, and Jimmy leaves. The sirens of the four motorcycle escorts say it's over.

"Habitat for Humanity, negotiating peace accords." The voice is still speaking, though much more softly.

Funny, the sirens are coming back.

Maybe the President forgot something.

I'll tell him this time to watch out for that *aya*tollah with the dead-soul eyes.

The voice whispers, "He didn't let the fact that he was in office only one term keep him from going on and doing great things."

Maybe I better not tell him. Jimmy's achieving what he's going to achieve. It's life, gotta keep on rollin', like that big river, Columbia. How does that go? Columbia, roll on. The river must find the ocean. No turning back. Can't be any other way. It's the way it was, the way it is, the way it will be: It's all the same water.

Yes, but is poor Jimmy ever in for one surprise with those hostages.

The husky front tires of a red-trimmed white ambulance rocked to a stop. The doors swung open each side. Engine left running, the two paramedics in whites were out immediately, for on the ground, sprawled between sidewalk and grass of the curbyard was a fallen sparrow of a man.

A man whose advanced age was not readily apparent to these rescuers, but which in a synchronous play of time was expressed where the ribbed and grooved rubber of the front right tire met the street curb into whose concrete form mere decades ago was affixed a horse ring.

An indestructible horse ring for tying up the reins of that earlier horsepower that moved buggies when Irvington was the new Portland subdivision. The horse rings, mounted in curbs all over the neighborhood, were archaeology, yes, but exactly the detail that never failed to please the elder Pliny, who now lay on the ground.

In practiced motions, the two gently loaded the white-sheeted gurney with the stricken man for whom a finely postured woman standing close by had dialled 9-1-1, medical emergency, after the shock of seeing, from her parlor window, this familiar walker past her place collapse.

The gurney lifted and locked on the van bed, the driver paramedic moistened a cloth to clean blood from Pliny's nose. "Took a nasty fall, but look at this old guy's color."

His partner got busy, attached monitors, slipped a yellow plastic mask over Pliny's face.

Ah, fresh air. Now where have I been? Maybe I keep my eyes closed, I can see Jimmy Carter one more time.

"His heart's strong, look at that," the driver said.

The woman from the sidewalk moved closer, beaming relief the dear man would make it.

The driver studied then dropped a paper chart, its tail spewing out of a recording device. His partner flipped on a dashboard speakerphone, punched up Emanuel Hospital ER.

"Hey, guys, we got an O on the way."

I must have taken a tumble and now I'm going to the hospital. Pliny's eyes opened.

"What O?" a voice crackled from the speakerphone.

"What, you new? O, open mouth, a pulse. Q, tongue out and gone, man. This one's an O and we're rolling."

The driver hesitated closing the other half rear-door and the two pairs of eyes met. Pliny remained among the living.

A professional, though, the driver walked once more to where he found his client, noticed a bulky transistor radio, the leather case half worn away, and picked it up, giving it to the shotgun paramedic. "Don't make them like this anymore. Keep it with the personal effects."

At Emanuel, a medical team held Pliny forty-eight hours for observation, ordering test panel after test panel with not one positive, told Pliny he was lucky to not have broken bones and then discharged him.

Back in his Old Portland Style bungalow, in the dining room, he enjoyed a hot meal of chicken nuggets and gravied mashed potatoes and talked with his caregiver from Daily Bread, Maud.

"So what did they say at the hospital?" His putting away the food pleasantly surprised her.

"Nothing. Those doctors told me keep doing what I'm doing, everything works fine."

"They have any idea why you blacked out?"

"Oh, I wrote it down here, somewhere." He spooned up the last of the mashed potatoes, licked his lip, and eased out a folded paper from his shirt pocket. "Says 'possible ischemic event.' But those are just doctor words to get Medicare to pay up. I fainted, that's all."

"You were lucky."

"Yep, a bloody nose and this dream I can't shake out of my mind."

"What dream?"

"Oh, a crazy dream about when President Carter slept here in Irvington. I ever tell you I met him then, back in seventy-eight?"

"No."

"Anyway, got me thinking. I used to hope that when my time was up, after all these years I put into living, things might be decent with the world, maybe people would even be singing those high notes of Beethoven's Ninth Symphony. Well, you see, now, I have to settle for reality—could be one little tuba toot. I'm taking the river of life as it comes. That's how Jimmy did it and that's how he still does it, bless him."

"Your appetite, Pliny. This is the first time you finished before I left."

"You bet. I want to get out, shake up my bones. Sun's shining. Did I tell you the forsythia are in bloom this week?"

Tall Maud stepped around the table, patted him on the back. She had a meal for her next client to deliver. She had to leave now and see Pliny then tomorrow.

VALENTINES IN VALHALLA

Trinity had waited for the two burly deliverymen who drove up—ROSCOE'S APPLIANCES—FREE DELIVERY!—late one Saturday afternoon in February. With a nine-year-old's patience, she would now wait for them to leave.

Her fast-talking dad, Steve, knowing the truck would eventually arrive, had gone downtown, looking up stuff at Central Library. His parting words, after lunch, were no more than: "You guys, be sure you read the instructions first."

All this because Wednesday at dinner, Steve said, "Guess what? This Saturday, a new dishwasher's coming. Bought it on my lunch hour."

Head down, Trinity had rolled her eyes and kept nibbling away at the mixed greens salad she'd helped her mom, JoBecca, make to go with pizza. Also at the table, Bailey, Trinity's younger and only sibling, skipped the salad and ate slices of stringy pizza.

"Why? What we got's perfectly fine, hon," JoBecca said.

"No, that racket," Steve said. "I want to relax when I'm home."

Remembering that disagreement between her parents kept Trinity cooped up in her room, her Saturday on hold: She didn't want to hear JoBecca speculating anymore whether they needed the new dishwasher. She truly didn't understand what made her dad go buy the thing and she didn't want to take sides. Not really.

The plan for the day was, if the men ever left, JoBecca would take her to Fabrika. They'd buy some cool appliqués for her new jeans, then pick up Bailey, who had spent the night at Lindsey's.

Trinity sighed. All she heard was grunts downstairs from the deliverymen struggling with the new dishwasher. She hated waiting. She flopped back on the bed and squinted at the first row of her Dolls Around the World atop the dresser. The East Indian rani, the Japanese geisha, the Mexican señorita, the Argentinean gaucho girl, and the French mademoiselle. These costumed treasures and sixty more came with Trinity from Chattanooga last year, when Steve, back from a telecom convention in Reno, announced their lives could only improve a "whole bunch" because he was a new district sales manager at a "gold mine" company and they were moving to Portland, Oregon. So she and the dolls moved.

Just then, JoBecca came in, wearing an orange Vols sweatshirt and wheat jeans. Trinity sat up, so as not to look obviously bored. "Whew, that took a bit longer than I like," her mom said. "Now, 'fore I disremember it and long as we're makin' room for your father's sensitivities, did I tell you practicing after dinner's a no-no?"

"Mom, our concert's in two weeks."

"Trinity, practice first thing you get home. Do that one thing for me, okay?"

"But why is it always Steve this, Steve that? We get this new dishwasher 'cause the old one bothers him. Now I can't play my *flute*?"

"Honey, I don't understand it all myself, but Steve needs his peace and quiet once he's home. It's like he'll be a ball of energy most times and can sell to beat the band. Your father *is* a terrif salesman. But he comes home, his tires can go flat, believe you me. Say, why am I telling you all this? You're just a kid."

JoBecca waved Trinity out of the room. They had to hustle and get to Fabrika before closing. Her mom was grins and seemed relieved to tell someone about this private worry.

Trinity picked at a hangnail, waiting for JoBecca to unlock the car. And before they backed out the driveway, she said, "Mom, I'll practice like Steve wants, four to five, but I can't help you with dinner anymore."

"That's okay." JoBecca flicked on the wipers to clear the drizzled windshield. "It's a phase he's going through. Maybe there's some medication."

"But why is he like this?" Her dad's latest demand about flute playing had unsettled Trinity and she had no pleasant choice except to go along.

JoBecca maneuvered down narrow 22nd, pausing at Stanton, an intersection with no stop signs like most of Irvington. She checked both ways and only mid-block, before Knott, replied: "See, your father has always been looking for something better. Like the move out here was gonna be his Valhalla or some such. Then we get here, time goes by, and he's thinking that Oregon is not the place. That's what he's looking up at the library: places to move."

"The dishwasher, same thing," JoBecca kept on. "It might bother him in six months if something else doesn't get him first. I don't know. Your father's one complicated man. Let's leave it at that."

"Oh," Trinity said, pleased her mom was telling her more, but unsure what it meant. They sped up Broadway to Fabrika over in the Hollywood District not talking, wipers on intermittent, and JoBecca absentmindedly humming along with the easy-listening love songs of Radio Ten-Ten, as if everything, one day, would be A-OK.

The following Tuesday, in her room, where the bed was made and even the study desk organized, Trinity gave Bailey the big-sister scoop on valentines. They sorted through a heap of cards about them on the bed.

"This is nice," Bailey said, cradling a red heart-shaped card, white-filigreed about its edges. "Who's this for?"

"Don't know yet. I need a list to see who deserves the best valentines."

"I like this one." Bailey held out an especially wide card with two hearts, siamesed side-by-side. "Who gets this one?"

Trinity clicked a ballpen, opening a Pee Chee folder with a tablet tucked under the right flap. "If Paige hadn't said that stuff about Tai's clothes, she said Tai's family bought at Goodwill, she would be near the top on my list, but that was bad, really bad. Don't you think so?"

Bailey's dark, bowl-cut locks framed a quizzical face. "What's Goodwill?"

"Oh, it's the place that sells what people give away. Everything kinda looks, you know, out-of-date."

"I wouldn't give Paige a valentine."

Trinity kept scribbling line after line and was, in fact, on a second page. From her assortment pack of fifty valentines, she might give out thirty, Bailey could choose from the other twenty, and they could save any leftovers for next year. Trinity clicked the ballpen. Who else? Who else?

"There, thirty names," she said, holding the two pages apart.

"Any boys?" Bailey said.

"Uh-uh, boys are icky."

Bailey leafed through the valentines, starting two piles.

"Now, I copy these over in the right order," Trinity said. "Then I pick the thirty best valentines and put them in order too. So Libby gets the best valentine and then Reed gets the next best. Isn't that easy? And you can have the leftovers, twenty of 'em."

"But those are the worst valentines. Can't I have some good ones?"

"Bailey, they're free. You didn't buy them. I did."

Just then both sisters heard their mom quit the kitchen and go to the foyer. The doorbell had chimed.

"I'm home early," their dad said. "Come out here, see what I got."

"Oh, Steve, can't you bring it inside?"

"C'mon, c'mon, no hints, everybody gets surprised."

"Trinity, Bailey," JoBecca called upstairs. "Come down and see your father's surprise."

The sisters reluctantly abandoned the valentines semi-sorted in two piles and marched through hallway, down stairs, and out the open front door. Beyond the knee-high boxwood hedge, on the twin strips of driveway concrete, showroom polished, sat an SUV, a silver BMW one.

"Had to have this baby," Steve said.

JoBecca said nothing and studied Steve more than the car.

Trinity saw her dad stop smiling like he had expected people to be happier. "Can we go for a ride?" She guessed Steve was waiting to hear that. "Please."

"Steve, our vacation. Remember? We haven't even bought the tickets." JoBecca's voice sounded like she had more questions.

"Why worry," he said. "This baby, oh, she goes anywhere. Four-wheel drive. All the time. No road. No problem."

"Cozumel, you didn't forget?" JoBecca said.

"Cozumel? Easy. This baby's a BMW, nothing stops BMW." Steve laced the fingers of both hands, his ring finger sporting the new key ring, his hands clasping the key fob and car keys like the secret to happiness for once, at last, was his.

"Steve, we're not gonna be cooped up in this car two weeks. We only have two weeks. I want to fly there. *En-ti-en-de u-sted*?"

Trinity wanted to say again, *What about riding in the new car?* but she knew that her mom was too upset. She looked to Bailey, but her sister was by the car, too short to peek in the tinted windows and see anything, but content to daub her fingers over its chrome, as if she knew that she might leave the first human marks on the car's silvered edges.

Trinity caught her sister's eye and ignored the standoff between her parents. "Bailey, let's go finish up the valentines." Her sister, as ever, looked puzzled. Trinity gave her a hard squint. Bailey had to know then to leave their parents alone.

Friday the thirteenth, the day before Valentine's Day, came to Irvington School and Trinity and others, almost all girls, were busy giving out valentines. Tucked in her JanSport book bag, Trinity, mid-afternoon, had heart-emblazoned cards by the dozens, possibly more than she had handed over to Kezia, to Reed, to Camela, to all the others straggling on the way to school, chatting by lockers in the hall, doodling in the classroom, running on the playground, or laughing in the lunchroom.

Then, impossibly, Clayton, the moon-eyed guy she had worked at ignoring since sometime before Christmas, came up to her with an envelope. She winced. He looked even wider in his baggy cargo pants. "Here," he said. "This is for you." His words spilled together like he'd waited all day for the moment.

"Thank you, Clayton," she said, ready to hurry on. But he stood there, blocking her, the moon eyes filled with expectation. She felt uncomfortable. Did he want her to open the valentine right there? "I'll open all my cards," she said, "when I get home. This will be one of the first." Clayton didn't budge and seemed planted in the hallway when she sidestepped him and rushed away, as if determined to make up for some lost seconds.

Trinity's thumb bent the envelope. Boys were so icky! Clayton was not the worst, but all of them were rough and jumped about like puppy dogs. Girls, naturally, were cool and calm. Yes, girls were calm. Girls were simply more mature.

She'd show Clayton's card to Bailey at home. A valentine from a boy. It really was Friday the thirteenth.

After she got home, the two sisters sat on the bed in Trinity's room, a day's haul of valentines gathered on the slipcover.

"Here, this is the worst one. A valentine from a boy," Trinity said, unwilling to open the envelope from Moon Eyes.

"Ooooo—a boy!" Bailey took the card, almost tearing the envelope flap to uncover what might be an expansive declaration of love. Clayton had printed no more than TRINITY above the message, "Valentine's comes once a year and I'll be yours all year long!" and beneath, also in all caps, his name.

"Gee, now you have a boyfriend," Bailey said.

Trinity busied herself tearing open another valentine.

Suddenly, the phone was ringing and Trinity dashed downstairs to pick up in the kitchen, but it stopped. Her mom was on the remote in the parlor. "Steve, what's wrong?" Trinity froze. Unseen, behind the kitchen wall, she wanted to hear more.

"Why don't you get yourself a physical? Could be that it's something else." Trinity kept still, moving nothing more than her eyes.

"You sound like you've been thinking about this too much. I didn't know." Her mom's words were hesitant and seemingly heavy with pain.

Trinity eyed with longing the wall phone next to her. She could only hear one side of the conversation. She leaned on the wall, her hands balled up, and breathing so softly she might as well have been one of the Dolls Around the World grown life-size.

"I can talk with the girls. Or do you want me to wait?"

Trinity gazed down at her fingernails curled into the heel of a palm. This was serious, really serious. Things were bothering Steve so much.

"Okay, I'll get all that together. You rest well, you hear? And don't worry 'bout the girls, I'll tell them you're away for a while."

Her eyes and nostrils widened; she pursed her lips. Her dad was staying away tonight. She unclinched her hands and pressed them flat against her legs and kept leaning on the wall.

Clunk. Her mom had put down the receiver. Trinity's legs were quivery as if she should be sneaking out the kitchen. But she had to stay put; she had to be busy. She sprang to the humming fridge, opened the door, keeping an ear cocked toward the hallway.

No Dr Pepper. Nothing else she liked. That was okay—JoBecca rushing up the stairs meant Trinity could now safely tiptoe out.

In the second-floor hallway, muffled sobbing came from her parents' room. Then she surprised Bailey, who evidently had been reading *every* one of Trinity's valentines.

"Why are you sneaking around?" Bailey asked.

"I'm practicing. Practicing being quiet as a ghost," Trinity said, not wanting her sister to know what was probably the awful truth about their dad.

"Oh," Bailey replied, going back to the valentines.

That night the Bemis family dinner was subdued owing to fast-talking Steve's absence for something other than the usual business trip. JoBecca was open about what was happening and told the girls he wasn't feeling right and needed to be away from the family until he felt better.

JoBecca dished out some steaming ravioli and launched into how she understood manic depression, which was her best guess on what was with Steve.

"I get like that too," said Trinity. "My feelings go up and down. I never know what's next."

"Well, don't you start in buying a new car and then two days later the dealer's gotta take it back."

Trinity poked the ravioli with her fork tines. She was not hungry, certainly not spicy-tomato-sauce hungry. So her dad had lost control of money. Her mom's joke was wrong. "Are we going to be poor?" she asked, trying to be serious.

"No, dear, we're just going to economize all the way 'round. We'll be okay."

"But how long will Steve be like this?" Trinity asked.

"Don't know. At least a few months. That's how I'd guess it."

"I hope he gets all better real soon," Bailey said.

Then JoBecca asked how the schoolwork was going.

After dinner, Trinity helped her mom with the dishes, cleaning plates of uneaten ravioli and lettuce and scrub rinsing them for the new dishwasher and, with those chores done, realized, yet again, Steve's fast-talking voice was gone.

"Mom, it's okay if I practice my flute now, huh?"

"Sure, go ahead," JoBecca said.

Trinity was about to tackle Sonata #2 by Bach for an uncounted time, when her mom stopped in the doorway. She laid the flute across her lap.

"Your birthday's almost here."

"The big one-*O*." Trinity chuckled.

"Well, I was thinking that we'd promised to buy you a flute."

"I picked one out at Piedmont Music."

Her mom, who seemed more tired than usual, slumped against the door frame. "That's the problem, part of it, anyway. I know what your heart's set on, a new flute. But it's gonna be difficult to budget anymore."

Suddenly, Trinity felt her birthday had lost its specialness. Then she remembered the money she'd been saving for college, part of it from her grandparents. "What about my savings? I have nearly enough for a flute."

"I don't know. You think Grandma and Grandpa Bemis would be okay with that?"

"If I had my own flute, I'd get really good and I might win a college scholarship worth a lot of money. They'd like that."

JoBecca stood away from the doorframe and gave her daughter a look of wry consent.

Trinity kept at the Bach for an hour, until eight-thirty.

As always, she swabbed out the flute, swabbed it dry. She saw Bailey had left the unused valentines on her desk in one heap. The top one pictured a school girl, blonde, pigtails, not unlike herself, clutching a long-stemmed rose in one hand and said,

"Roses are roses, blues are blues." Inside, "And there's only one of yous. Be my valentine, please!"

Trinity liked it: funny but sincere. She flipped through the rest and didn't find another she liked as well.

Tomorrow was really Valentine's Day and she still could give it to someone. JoBecca? Mom needed a valentine with the rough day she'd had.

Or Steve? Her brow furrowed at that idea of her father alone somewhere, beer in hand, maybe watching TV, something like Frasier, but definitely not happy.

She would give both JoBecca and Steve valentines. But the one for Steve came first.

She grabbed a ballpen from the desk drawer. The one that wrote in red. On the envelope front, she printed DAD. Big well-formed letters. He would know at a glance it was from her, not Bailey. Then inside the card, she wrote "Dear Dad," and below, "Be my valentine, please! I miss you terribly, hope you come back real soon. Love, Trinity."

She shut the card, began slipping it in the envelope and paused. The girl clutching the single yellow rose reminded her of enormous beds of roses in Riverpark back in Chattanooga and something with Steve that happened when she was only eight.

She was playing on a merry-go-round in Riverpark overlooking the Tennessee River where it runs through the city. A hot May afternoon, the busy cicadas in the tall cottonwoods could be heard everywhere.

On that merry-go-round, at one time, were at least six kids, all taking turns running beside it for more speed, jumping back on like Trinity had for the thrill: hanging on the outside vertical bars, her skinny frame leaning out, her blonde braids dangling, her eyes dancing in a world gone upside down with a stomach-turning centrifugal charge. When Trinity had enough, when she decided to jump off, she was so wobbly she couldn't walk straight.

The grass and all else spun. She didn't know where to find her mom and dad and Bailey. She lurched this way, then that.

Suddenly, partly hidden in the thick blades of springy St. Augustine grass—and she was about to step on it—a lifeless, huge crow, its ruffled wings spread funny.

She screamed.

A scream to anyone anywhere to help, please. The crow's eye socket was empty and small brown ants streamed in and out of its open, shiny beak. She choked trying to scream again.

Then suddenly, without a word, Steve was there, his big powerful hands pressed her ribs and lifted her straightaway, so her head nestled safely against his. "That's nothing t'worry about," he said as calmly as if teaching her to throw a baseball.

Her heart ran wild. She was breathless. But the world no longer spun.

Across the springy grass, back to the wooden picnic table, he carried his rescued daughter. "Our Trinity, she was about to trip on a poor dead bird." She knew then Steve would help with the awful things in the world.

She looked again at the card she'd written and began to cry. Her dad was still strong for her. She would ask her mom about seeing Steve tomorrow, Valentine's Day, to give him the card. She missed him already.

Besides, he needed some cheering up. She couldn't think of what else to do. The rest of the unused cards she would show Bailey, who was in the family room with the TV on. See if she wanted to send a valentine too. But first, she had to give the tears time to stop.

She looked at the card again and saw a tear marked the valentine for Steve. The tear would dry but leave a stain. She choked back fresh tears: She would have to do a new valentine. But if Steve saw a tear from sadness on the card, he'd know she missed him. She could leave it. A smile flickered across her lips.

As Saturday turned out, Trinity did not personally deliver the tear-stained valentine. Something about Steve being away from Portland for the day. JoBecca let her mail it, though, which she did, unsure it would ever reach him.

The only sure thing in Trinity's life was that Irvington Elementary School's orchestra would play Friday night. And then too quickly the hour of reckoning was upon Trinity, who sat onstage with the other orchestra kids, in their dressy best, bright spotlights haloing their heads. The Sonata #2 score she shared with the other flutist, Leigh, rested on a music stand tray between them. Trinity fussed about, realigned the flute sections, held it out sideways, silvery mouthpiece at her lips, and tapped tone holes and key levers to be sure her fingers, despite onstage jitters, still moved. In front, violin players plucked and bowed strings, tuning up with a peg twist or two.

Beyond the stage, in the auditorium dimness, shadowy people kept filing in for seating. Trinity squinted and hoped she and the other kid musicians would not let so many people down.

Mr. Haflund, the orchestra teacher, who also played clarinet in the Oregon Symphony, walked out frontstage, talking softly, asking them to all check that their sheet music was at the beginning of the Bach sonata.

Still facing them, he touched his black bow tie, tightly knotted on the white shirt he wore with his professional tux, then smartly turned on his heel, faced the audience and bowed deeply.

Trinity sat erect, her flute at the ready.

Then before she could search the audience again for JoBecca and Bailey, the instrumental voices were chorusing forth, Mr. Haflund waving baton up and down, coaxing the violins in the quiet beginning of the piece.

Then came the flute duet. Trinity plunged in, playing as she had for months; she and Leigh playing as tight, as together as they had in practice that morning. Mr. Haflund beamed and directed baton sweeps toward them, as if adding the final grooming touches to the run of notes they had flawlessly delivered.

Trinity caught her breath. The flutes were incredible and they had only to do it once more, a reprise near the end.

Resting with flute in lap, military-pride posture, Trinity squinted past the stage lighting. She had yet to see JoBecca and

Bailey and the light varied too much. Some faces she saw, others were indistinguishable.

Then her eyes grew wide. For a few rows back sat Steve, gazing her way, blankly, as if he hadn't noticed her. She stared hard because he had dyed his hair black, shoe-polish black. Was it that he didn't want anybody to recognize him, dying his blond hair this awful black? But his face, his eyes, his nose, his mouth—that was her dad. She knew that. She leaned forward to see if, by moving, he might pick her out.

He didn't. He kept looking up at the orchestra as if he were also looking right through her. Trinity bit her lip.

Was he pretending not to see her? Why was he doing this? And, worst, his hair looked bad.

Trinity kept giving Steve a hard look, but nothing became clearer. Suddenly, Leigh was playing the reprise beside her and the flute was still in Trinity's lap.

She hurriedly brought the cold metal of the mouthpiece to her lips.

Omigod. She had messed up.

Only after the concert, did Trinity find JoBecca and Bailey. She asked her mom if she had seen Steve and she said, No, he wasn't there. Trinity wanted to tell her mom about Steve and the hair dyed black, but she had so many questions, she had to think about it more, it was so odd. Anyway, she was glad the concert was over.

For days to follow, Trinity could not let go the memory of Steve with black hair. What did his being there mean? That he missed her? That he got her valentine and wanted to see her? She didn't know. She decided Steve wanted to see her and Bailey and JoBecca again, but moving back in with them wouldn't work. The only way he could see them was to find them somewhere and wear his disguise, hair dyed black or sunglasses or a floppy hat or something. Then he wouldn't have to talk about his problems. Trinity's stomach was a knot of worry that Steve was gone for good and might not get well.

In her room, the halves of the flute case open flat on the bed, she took out the tubular sections and joined them, meditatively. All her practice had paid off in a way. She had seen Steve again. But she didn't know if that was the end, with his disguise and everything. She just didn't know.

Then JoBecca walked in. "Why are you sitting in the dark?" Above, the light fixture was dim.

"I was going to play my flute."

"With these lights out?"

"I don't know anything about putting in new ones."

"You're right. Changing light bulbs was a Steve specialty. On that ladder, I don't even know where he kept it."

"It's in the garage."

"No, no. Don't need it. Tomorrow I'll call us an electrician, have him come out, change the light bulbs. Oh, joy, not having a man around."

JoBecca, shoved her hands in her loose housedress and raised her shoulders, as if the future were up for grabs.

Trinity remembered exactly how the wooden ladder rested by the shelving deep in the garage. "Mom, let's ask Steve to come by and change the lights, can't we do that, please?"

"I dunno, probably he wouldn't mind a short while. I'll call and see."

Her mom left and Trinity held her flute out sideways, brought the mouthpiece to her lips, pursed in the practiced embouchure.

She would look at his hair closely. If he had not washed it all out, his roots would show.

Her eyes fairly danced to the black trills inked in bunches across the pages of the score displayed on the music stand and then, once again, Trinity was playing Bach.

RED BALL

Red ball. Yellow block. Blue cone. Among these objects, each light, plastic, hollow, an infant struggled. A soft flannel cover disguised the tough, water-resistant mat of the playpen in which, belly-up, the infant waved puffy arms and then slammed its right hand down. Two parents gazed upon their firstborn, now fourteen weeks along.

"Should it be like that, on its back?"

"Dunno. Can't remember if it's the back or stomach that's bad."

"Great, SIDS, fifty-fifty chance."

"What do you want to do, call Dr. Townsley? Now? Nine-thirty?"

"Nah, I'll do a Web search."

The infant seemed blissfully beyond any talk of a life threat. Then, for its own reason it pushed—did not strike—its right hand on the flannel cover, as if trying to lever and roll its body stomachward. But the effort stalled. The short arm of the infant could not change where its body lay one whit.

Intense, more focussed than weeks before, the eyes of the infant took in its parents. What did it know with those blue, watery eyes? This was the guessing game for the parents: What did the infant see? What did the infant feel? And most important, What did the infant want?

As if giving up on the effort, the infant stopped pushing its right fist to the mat and instead raised overhead, to the hovering parents, the chubby hand with a crooked forefinger no longer than a crayon stub. The forefinger pointing upward to what it saw.

Two faces. One face on taller body with glass spectacles in front of eyes. Face with short hair. Hair color like curtain sunlight. Mouth, turned down at corners, opens, closes. "V guvax ur'f ybbxvat ng zr."

Mouth in other face on shorter body does not open, close. Thick lips, glossy red, smile. Long hair falls to shoulders, hair color like curtain sunlight too.

On mat, neck and back hurt. Head and body cannot turn over on mat. Taller body, shorter body can pick up body here. Neck, back hurt.

Both faces stop smiling. Hold up arm and hand and finger to touch face on shorter body, face with long hair. Cannot reach face. Face bends over close. Finger cannot reach face.

Mouth in closer face opens, closes. "Jung qbrf ur jnag? Ur whfg unq uvf sbezhyn."

Face moves away. Finger cannot touch face. Face moves further away. Neck and back still hurt. Arm, hand, finger pointing high at face, cannot touch. Bring back hand to face, bring both hands to face, now warm. WAAAAAHHHHH. Wet tears on warm face. Both hands hold face. WAAAAAHHHHH.

Two faces up there with mouths turned down at corners. "Qba'g cvpx uvz hc."

WAAAAAHHHHH.

Finger cannot touch face up there. Hands of shorter body do not reach down and pick up body. Arms and hands beside body wave up and down. Faces up there frown.

Faces on bodies up there turn around and only hair on heads up there shows. Bodies leave. Light in room leaves. Darkness falls here.

WAAAAAHHHHH.

Face here wet with tears. Neck, back still hurt. Red ball, yellow block, blue cone go away in darkness.

Eyes open. Body sits strapped in car seat held by seat belt to rear seat of auto. Moving, moving. Other side of glass window, building, big truck, another auto, streetlight pole, utility wire, cloud, tree, tree, patch of blue sky, plastic sign for store, billboard. Moving, moving. Two bodies in front seat of auto have hairy head tops and one with shorter hair turns sideways. Mouth opens, closes.

"Ur frrzf gb rawbl gur evqr fb sne."

"Gung'f tbbq."

Moving, moving. Stomach feels bad. Moving makes stomach feel bad. Moving, moving. Past window glides auto, auto, auto, truck, bus, spangled white cloud and faraway blue sky, electric wire drooping between pole, pole, pole. Then auto slows, stops. Stomach feels really bad.

"Waaaaahhhhh."

The auto halted at a traffic intersection, and the father, wrist topping the steering wheel, gave the mother an I-told-you-so glance. Earlier that week, they had disagreed about whether to accept the evening's dinner invitation if they didn't have, didn't know, a sitter.

"What's with that kid?"

The mother turned and in the car seat, the swaddled baby was strapped in tight as if he were an astronaut ready for a spaceflight launch. His nose, a facial bump with the smallest of nostrils, crinkled. He had stopped crying, yet his eyes kept an intensity suggesting he might not have finished.

"He's hungry." She was guessing. Her husband frowned and he pulled away from the intersection. Everything with baby was in the back seat: diapers, bottles of formula, the whole change bag. She thought forty-five minutes across town wouldn't be a big deal, but her neighbor Stephanie had warned first trips were always a trial.

"I can't pull over."

"Waaaaahhhhh." The infant waved his arms in the air as if struggling to be free of the straps. "Waaaaahhhhh." The mother saw her husband clinch the steering wheel and knew before long he would turn his irritation on her. It was only a baby and yet this new bundle of life could bring them to bicker with just a cry.

"You have to pull over," she said. The face back there, no bigger than her hand, was wrinkled pink. "His bag's in the back seat."

"Okay, but next time, we're gonna think about a sitter." She had been so busy since coming home from the hospital, the thought of who might eventually baby-sit had escaped her. But Trinity, down the block on 18th, might like earning the money. She always seemed to come by anyway with various sales pitches: fancy chocolates, fun-run pledges, magazine subscriptions—all raising money, Trinity said, for her school. Yes, and Trinity was about the right age, ten.

The next day, the infant was back in the playpen, surrounded by the familiar red ball, yellow block, and blue cone. The infant slept on its back, entangled in a small blanket, the fingers of one hand in its mouth.

The mother came in, saw the sleeping infant, the tangle of blanket. She bent over to fix the blanket and make the baby more comfortable. When she did this, the infant stirred.

"Waaaaahhhhh." The infant seemed ready for another crying jag. At times, she didn't know what to make of his discomfort. His needs appeared simple. Eating, sleeping, diaper changes.

And she had taken care of those needs—he'd been sleeping, his diaper was okay, and he ate within the hour. What else could make him cry?

"Waaaaahhhhh."

When he took to crying, the one thing the infant did not want was to be ignored. And yet the mother did not want to always give him attention. If she did, she reasoned, before long the baby (and future adult) would believe the world worked on whining.

So, she decided to keep him as unspoiled as she could manage and hope that would make him more independent. Despite this resolve, she did bend down this time and pick up her cuddly human. For, to be fair, it was she who disturbed him, untangling his blanket. But she was getting systematic about when to answer his cries and when not to.

But this wasn't time to choose: She had disturbed him.

She held him close, feeling the warmth from such a small body.

"Waaaaahhhhh."

Cooing him soft nonsense words, words that other times lulled him to sleep, she walked to an end table and retrieved a formula bottle.

Inverted, the bottle's white content flowed to the orangy tip that she let his saliva-rich lips guzzle, his lips so small that they seemed not much bigger than the nipple itself.

He suckled the latex nipple and as if to affirm his contentment, he raised the free arm that was away from her and with his hand and forefinger pointed upward at her face as if he also wanted to touch her too.

Suck. Suck. Warm liquid, good taste. Fills mouth. Swallow, goes down throat. Suck, suck. Long hair, color like curtain sunlight. Fingers reach, hold hair. Warm liquid in throat, in stomach. Suck. Suck.

Face with long hair, color like curtain sunlight, swings and moves while suck, suck, more warm liquid in throat, in stomach.

Suck. Suck. More warm liquid in throat, in stomach. Full in stomach. Full in throat. Stomach hurt. Too much warm liquid. Pressure in throat. Cannot suck, suck.

Nipple in mouth. Cannot suck, suck. Too full. Shake head. Nipple in face, nipple at lips. Shake head. Too much warm liquid. WAAAAAHHHHH.

Pressure in throat. Pressure in stomach. Pressure in chest. Too much warm liquid. Nipple and bottle go away. Swing, swing,

to and fro. Hand pat back. Pressure inside. Hand pat back. Pressure different. Pressure moves. Pressure moves up throat.
    BLOOOSHHH. BLOOOSHHH. Wet lips, warm liquid goes out wet lips.
    "Tbbq onol, tbbq onol."
    Hand pat back. Hand pat back.
    Hands lower body to playpen mat, then body goes away, returns with towel. Hands use towel to wipe liquid off lips and then face with long hair goes away. Darkness falls in room.
    WAAAAAHHHHH.
    In darkness, no red ball.
    WAAAAAHHHHH.

    The mother gave up expecting things would soon change. And they didn't. For her baby was learning quickly to demand. Whenever he was hungry, he cried. Oh, how he howled. And nothing as blatantly deceptive as a pacifier would stop the bawling if he were hungry. So out came one of the formula bottles she vigilantly had at the ready when the keening call came. And if she was unlucky enough to run out of bottles, that was the pits, something she did only once.

    He would gulp the liquid down—always too fast—as if famished and she knew he was swallowing all the more air. Then, bloated, he needed to burp. He would take to crying again and a pacifier was no answer. She had to lift him and begin coaxing his stomach to release the trapped air. She'd bounce him lightly on her arm, his screaming face on the towel at her shoulder and she would wait for that *bloosh*. Invariably, the burp seemed to startle him and stop the crying. She'd clean him off and bounce him in her arms to enjoy, if only for minutes, the welcome calm.

    But before long, with the exertion of eating, then struggling at the dogged compulsion to burp, he seemed to be exhausted, about to drop off into the unknown world, sleep. With this exhaustion came resistance. He fought sleep with more crying. Only then did the pacifier work. Munching away on the orangy nipple, the eyelids would droop and then relief, he was asleep.

When he awoke hours later, the cycle would start anew. And he awoke anytime during the twenty-four hours of each and every day. But the mother found she could endure, knowing that Friday, she would have an evening respite of at least six hours. Trinity was coming to baby-sit for the first time. The mother yearned for that relief and was all the more grateful Trinity lived but a few doors away.

The parents were gone and Trinity, who the mother learned had done a fair amount of baby-sitting, was particularly anxious to have a good time with the baby. She was warned, somewhat indirectly, he might need a lot of attention. They were in the family room, the playpen a center stage, and Trinity studied a stack of CDs by the stereo. There was something about music and babies. They liked music.

She sifted the CDs, saw a Scott Joplin, dropped it in the player. The infant who had been quiet up to now, who seemed to be taking in the new face—hers—grinned with the rousing melody of "Maple Leaf Rag." The music animated him. He raised a leg and let it happily drop.

Trinity was pleased that this baby, too, took a liking to music. She bent over the playpen to share more closely his soft gurgling. His mouth dribbled with happy gurgles.

"Wanna dance, big guy?"

She reached in and clutched him close. He *was* her dance partner. They circled the room slowly. To each run of the piano, they stepped and bounced gently until they were back where they started. She put him down when a new song started; she felt he had enough excitement for the moment. He sat there, propped up against the wooden bars of the playpen.

The infant seemed to roll around—for he was not yet old enough to crawl—to face the wooden fence that confined him. And up went an arm, the hand and fingers extended in a grabbing gesture at one of the upright slats.

Hand holds wooden bar. Fingers squeeze smooth wood. Hand holds bar until fingers hurt, until fingers turn to wood and hand now part of wooden bar too. Body pulls back, rolls back to leave hand on wooden bar, leave it there. Body pulls harder so hand comes off and stays on wooden bar. Body keeps pulling, then hand comes loose from wooden bar.

WAAAAAHHHHH.

Arm still has hand. Hand won't come off and stay on wooden bar.

WAAAAAHHHHH.

Trinity picked another CD to play, but saw him struggling with the playpen, as if he wanted out or something. She bent over and gently scooted him next to the red ball at the center of the mat. His right arm went out, his hand seemingly drawn to the red object.

Red ball by blue cone. Two hands grab red ball, one to each side. Hold red ball tightly. Hands wave up and down. Red ball goes up and down. Body pulls away from red ball. Red ball moves too. Red ball can't stay like wooden bar. Red ball moves with hands, with arms, with body.

Hands go away from red ball. Red ball falls.

Then both hands grab red ball again. Hands wave up and down. Red ball goes up and down. More music. Wave red ball with loud music, up and down. Hands leave red ball and red ball goes up in air and hits wooden bar and rolls on mat.

WAAAAAHHHHH.

He was amazing, she decided: a two-handed toss of the red ball that bounced off the side of the playpen. Now, could he do it again? Trinity bent over and put the ball close by him. Immediately, his right hand shot out, his pointing finger tipping the ball.

Hands hold red ball and wave up and down. Red ball goes up and down. Hands go back and go forward and then let go of red ball. Red ball goes to wooden bars and bounces and hits mat.

Yellow block. Hands grab yellow block. Hold it tightly and wave up and down. Hands go back and then go forward. Yellow block goes to wooden bar, bouncing to mat like red ball. Yellow block hits red ball.

Hands, arms, body make red ball, yellow block move. Hands grab blue cone. Blue cone flies across playpen too. Hands, arms, body, all one. Hands stay with arms, body. Red ball, yellow block, blue cone do not stay with hands, move away. Hands, arms, body make red ball fly through air, hands grab red ball and wave up and down. Hands, arms, body, all one.

Body with face comes to playpen and puts red ball right before hands, arms, body. Hands, arms, body pick up red ball and wave up and down at wooden bars that do not stay with hands, do not move like red ball moves. Hands wave higher and let go red ball. Red ball flies up in air, above wooden bars, falls outside.

WAAAAAHHHHH.

"Home run, big guy!" Trinity yelled. She stooped down to pick up the red ball, still rolling, and all-smiles set it down next to her young charge, who waved his arms with an obvious frenzy to keep throwing the red ball.

Hands grab red ball and wave up and down and red ball flies above wooden bars.

Hands and arms and body want to throw red ball again. Hands and arms and body, all one want.

Hands and arms and body make red ball fly through air. Hands, arms, body, all one want. One want—I want. I make red ball fly through air. I want.

I want.

When the parents returned that evening, they had at first no inkling something had changed with the infant. The mother could not put her finger on it, but weeks later, she noticed he cried less and seemed more content in his playpen, tossing about toys. The red ball, especially, caught his eye. He delighted in hurling it out of the playpen. The mother, with some idle notion he might go to college on an athletic scholarship, rushed over every time his toss of the red ball cleared the playpen guardrail and restored his toy to its rightful place so he could keep up the practice.

Whenever she did this, he would gurgle happily and raise his arm and hand, with forefinger extended, as if he wanted to take the ball from her.

I want to make red ball fly and I grab red ball. Red ball flies out of playpen. Bounce. Roll. Stop. BA-BA-BA.

TIMED OUT

"You find this place okay?" he called to Averyl.

Averyl, who was the smile across the parking lot. Averyl, who on weekends dressed Sixties. Averyl, who agreed to see him Saturdays.

That was how it began a quarter to nine, one Saturday morning in the noisy parking lot beside Vancouver Lake, where he saw instantly the Oregon plates of his car and Averyl's stood out like cowlicks from those of Washington cars whose occupants were removing neon Frisbees, plaid woolen blankets, and pop-filled Igloo coolers with obvious intent to picnic and play under a sun-bleached blue sky.

"Love your shirt," said Averyl, as he reached to draw her close. On his lunch hour last Wednesday, he'd bought it over at Wonderland Mall. He requested the Mammoth-size letters for a custom T-shirt that said JUST SATURDAYS. Sixteen dollars for this T-shirt with a weighty message that confirmed, yes, Averyl, excitement in large letters, was in his schedule.

Fifty years along, he took a deep breath because Averyl, half his age at twenty-five, had, in their walking side by side, now put her arm snugly around his waist. And her hair—big and frizzy—smelled clean.

Until he parked by the lake, however, he had hidden the shirt beneath the spare tire in the trunk of the car so, among others, his wife, Kate, would not try to puzzle out what this had to do with his plan to work Saturdays.

The three hours with Averyl shot by and vanished. And after he and Averyl said good-byes, he had nothing more to live on than their promise to meet again next Saturday and he went back to Portland to Conifer Logic, the software shop, to phone Kate and see how her day was going. No one answered.

About four, he bagged any idea of finishing the code module he'd been writing, jumped in the car, and wended his way crosstown through Saturday afternoon traffic to Irvington, an old neighborhood of big maples and the blue-shuttered Colonial Revival where Kate, aerobics-thin, Gap denim overalls, black hair in a purposeful geometric cut—looking anything but the picture of a middle-aged matron who worked out of the home—stood in the driveway. And the way she moved, her posture tuned by the Alexander Technique, was grace itself. She was pulling heavy brown bags of groceries from the open hatchback.

"Need help?" he asked.

"There, the other bag, thanks."

"Hmmm." He perused contents: A paper-sleeved baguette; Braeburns; firm bananas; Romaine lettuce, its leaves girdled by a wired paper twist-tie tagged 100% ORGANIC. "Fertile eggs from free-range chickens—you musta been to Planet Foods."

"Can't say Albertson's has everything."

"Especially this. Hey, what's don-key?" he asked, taking a shot at the foreign words on a small brown bottle of capsules.

"Dong quai, thank you. It's a Chinese herbal mix."

He scratched his temple. Okay, he made the connect. Kate's change o' life and all the hormonal chaos. "Kinda ironic, don't you think, this dong something."

"You're being silly." He knew that not-amused smile of hers had an implicit demand for him to think of her needs just once. "Listen, Babs tried it, said it might work."

"With the hot flashes?" He beamed. He could've also asked about their love life going in the incinerator, so to speak, these past months, but that was sorta off-issue.

"Yeah, I need something," Kate said, carcinogenic estrogen pills not being on her list, thank you.

The next Friday morning, he entered the side door at Conifer Logic. Everywhere, keyboards clicked like code-hungry termites.

"What's the verdict?" he said, leaning into a cubicle where Duncan hunched over a stack of greenbar paper from a code dump. "You figure out why I'm not getting a refresh on the screen?"

"You betcha. Your indirect addressing was off," Duncan said, pointing to a page marked with a yellow Post-it. "Gotta reinitialize this loop every time through."

"And?"

"And you were writing to non-existent memory. The sucker timed out on you."

"And no refresh?"

"Not till you reinitialize."

That Duncan was a genius, he marvelled, leaving for his cubicle. He hummed upon reaching his desk and tapped his space bar to light up the workstation screen. The mailbox icon had a raised flag. An e-mail, he'd bet, from Averyl. But first, some coffee: Speed up those processor elements between his ears. He had a spec review meeting at ten.

Maybe he and Averyl were like code. He looked out the window at the blue May sky. The same clear weather of the spring when he was twenty-five, back from 'Nam, and falling in love with Kate. Later they married.

If love at twenty-five was the key, the event that initialized his love loop, then the loop would time out here in the Nineties and his subconscious, his whatever, was ready for a refresh, the big replay.

He sipped at the hot coffee, ready to log in and read e-mail. He was simply executing his code like any other man fifty years old, coming off the mat for another round. He almost chuckled at the thought, Kate was best then, and this time around, maybe it was Averyl.

He clicked on the mailbox icon. Message three was from Averyl at Viatronix:

Subject: Saturday

New plan. A friend asked me to house-sit her apartment tomorrow while she's over in Bend. Try calling at 12:30.

—*Kid Blast.*

He pushed the DELETE key with a glacial slowness. A mangled key sequence might trigger the upstairs printer for an unclaimed message sure to get some close readings.

That night, he slept only because imagining what was next from this retro-Sixties flower child was too much for him to bring up on his screen. Whatever, it would all be okay because Averyl had yet to relinquish her idealism, those years at U of O that let her effortlessly look past a detail like his marriage as an outmoded convention. He savored the hours with this natural woman that were almost upon him and finally switched off, exhausted, into sleep mode.

When he awoke the next morning, Kate slept beside him, head snug in the pillow dent, eyes closed, mouth open. Already past eight, he had to get out, get coffee, get moving to Averyl's. He rubbed Kate's freckled, smooth shoulder near the camisole strap. She yielded a groan of consciousness.

"I'm leaving. Off to work," he said.

"Huh." Her eyes opened, dreamily unfocussed. "What day's this? Isn't it Saturday?" She pulled the pillow tight against her ruddy cheek like she wasn't about to give up sleeping in.

"Yeah, I told you I've gotta put in the extra time, this Saturday, next Saturday, probably the next—"

"Till when?"

"I don't know. Q3?"

"You're always saying Q-this, Q-that."

"Big boss says we don't ship end of Q3, he's toast." He caressed her shoulder again.

"We don't do anything anymore on Saturdays together."

"I know. I miss that."

"You be long?"

"I don't know, depends."

After reshaping the pillow, Kate pulled the camisole strap over her exposed shoulder and he left.

He was on-time—as invariably he was—and he took it as a good omen that a blaze of sun topped the crown of an old maple across the street to catch his eye. Then he went inside the brick apartment building and rushed straight up two flights of stairs to 312.

The white door, overcoated with enamel paint, opened. She was barefoot and a vision, wearing a shift of translucent batik cotton. Her upturned palm led him in and he liked how ringlets of her hair slipped off the nape of her neck when she looked down to hide her Cheshire cat grin.

A jazz station rattled away on the stereo. His senses turned keen at the prompt of Averyl's perfume. And this was no ersatz apartment: French doors led to a dining room with a chandelier above a table, and each of the table legs was carved to a claw clutching a ball.

He pushed hair off Averyl's shoulder. "I didn't know if I was going to ever make it here."

"Same here. I almost called you at home," Averyl said with the mock emphasis he liked to hear. "I've been planning our little get-together." She grabbed his elbow, trying to steer him to the dining room, but he used his free arm to catch her for a single long kiss, ripe with a week's worth of anticipation.

"Over here. Over here." She tugged at his shirt sleeve.

He stepped into the dining room with her. He gave the table a quick look, a look he swept to Averyl, then to the table again. He was confused.

"Certainly don't serve coffee at this table," he said softly. His thumb and fingers clamped the thick, dark mahogany table edge.

Averyl had set out a magnum of Dom Perignon on ice, two empty champagne glasses, small boxes of wooden matches, two homemade cigarettes with ends twisted shut, and four unfamiliar capsules.

"Do you want me to explain," Averyl said with cheer, "the exact order, or do you prefer the surprise route?"

"A glass of champagne would be okay," he said, wracking his brain for a way to patch the situation.

"What?" Averyl leaned closer in disbelief.

"Why don't we each just have a glass of this champagne," he said somewhat louder. He cringed at the idea Averyl's free and natural spirit was most likely half drug-induced.

"No. No. Don't you see that you have to take these in the right order?" She spun the champagne on its bed of ice.

"Averyl, what are you getting at?"

She clasped the wet magnum and began untwisting its wire catch. "We have to take these in the right order, at the right time, to get the best effect." Averyl's eyes cut to him, quick with the challenge.

Talk about sex objects, being used. And he knew a nasty thing or two, didn't he, about drugs? Not to mention, he also had, eventually, to drive home.

He would be assertive: clear off the table with glass breaking everywhere and then take Averyl in one big hug. But his desire was dead.

No, it was Clark Gable in *Gone With the Wind*: The exit was less complicated if first you got them mad. "Why? Do I look like a guy who needs *this* for a little hardbody interaction?"

Averyl held up one of the capsules. "Worried what a little amyl nitrite will do for your old ticker, aren't you?"

He looked at the ceiling and then, after a deep breath, her. "Averyl, I think your attitude's gone nonlinear. Why don't we do each other a favor, wait until this emotional stackup's outta the way." His eyes widened at the finality of it all.

Averyl picked up a homemade cigarette. "I won't hold my breath about it. At least not until after you've gone and I've lit this joint."

He gave her the peace sign he remembered from the Sixties, when he protested the draft before going off to serve anyway, and then he left the building, drove for a couple of hours and went home.

After some killer food that night—Kate was, he had to admit, a wondrous cook—asparagus, shrimp over pasta, he was of a mind to relax from the trials of the day. So he grabbed the last Shiner Bock he'd brought back from the Texas trip and set himself up at the rolltop desk in the den. He slipped open the shell of his laptop and rollerballed to his sign-on macro. Some mindless Web surfing could only help the beer's effect in untangling this business about Averyl.

He sipped the heady beer, shirt-sleeved his lips dry. What was he thinking to get involved with her? God! And if she was perverse enough, no, burning-hemp stoned enough, she could just tell Kate what her husband had been up to.

He went to the GO line, typed *airwire.com/~averyl*. That's the last thing he needed: Kate after him about more than the amount of fiber in his diet.

He stared in disbelief. WELCOME TO AVERYL'S HOME PAGE. Ms. Wrong. Yep, Ms. Wrong. He clicked on the PERSONAL INTERESTS button. Hiking, classical music, reading? Where was the truth in advertising there? Why not drugs, drug-crazed sex, followed by more recreational drugs?

Another swallow of bubbly beer to settle the growing nausea about this smiley bitch blazing forth on his SVGA screen.

He kept navigating. He checked it all out. Clicked open the thumbnail shots, nothing special really, just pics of the fun girl next door so ready to take in some new unsuspecting fool. Not him. He'd learned. His feedback loop worked fine. Though now, having snuck around behind Kate's back, he felt like he'd been off Dumpster diving in ripe garbage and the problem was more than just coming up empty. Lose-lose.

His beer done, he needed another.

Last on one page was an option button: SEND E-MAIL TO AVERYL. He clicked, had no idea where to begin, and backed out.

Face it, this toothsome Ms. Big Hair was not good for him. Say, hypothetical, he'd given in to those bedroom eyes. Once funtime in LEGO-land was over, what was next? Nada. Minus zero.

Namely, what did they talk about last Saturday, the two of them walking the sandy beach of Lake Vancouver, dodging shrieking kids in wet bathing suits? It was mostly Averyl's big tease, big come-on.

"I wouldn't have any problem our relationship got intimate real soon," she said, a hand toying insouciantly with her hair.

"Oh, you're catching me unprepared." The image of a bare-assed tumble in the nearby woods left his mind in a dither.

"Don't worry, I'm a good Boy Scout, always prepared." Averyl unzipped her beltpack and was wiggling a strip of aluminum-encased Trojans. His smile broadened: Maybe he liked the idea of a younger woman taking the initiative.

"How long those last you?"

"Now, don't be getting the wrong idea. I'm not that sorta woman. I'm choosy." Averyl took his hand, swinging it. "A longtime married man, faithful, you gotta be close to zero risk, considering all that's out there."

"Zero risk, huh?"

"Hey, I like you for other reasons too." Averyl let go his hand and lightly punched his shoulder.

He should have known. She'd come right out and said it. Said he wasn't much more than a no-risk sex object that worked for her. How could today turn out differently? She wanted to use him like nothing more than a new Kleenex. God, he needed another beer.

He pushed out of the squawking desk chair and turning, his eyes refocussed with silent, wordless shock: Kate.

Her leaning against the doorframe, as if she'd been there for minutes. Her eyes on him—or—past him? The knowing smirk at her lips. His racing heart. *Thump. Thump.*

He fought the urge to look away. Didn't dare look back. He smiled wanly.

"You looked entranced," Kate said, her gaze micro-shifting back to the home-page harpy.

He wanted to ask, *How long you been standing here, sneaking up on me?* But he knew that remark would only get a scorched earth conflict going. He couldn't think—too much bus contention across his synapses. "Woman at work," he managed to say.

Kate squinted, said nothing.

Another wan smile. "Woman at work. Duncan helped Averyl put up that Web page. I wanted to see what they did." He sighed with instant relief at fabricating this cogent, rational explanation.

"How come you never mentioned—is it Averyl?—before?" Kate's face didn't quite have the relaxed look of acceptance, but it was getting there.

"She just joined us a few weeks ago," he said, amazed at his new-found gift of swapping truth for fiction, on the fly yet. "Excuse me, I was headed out for another beer." His thumb lifted her chin, he brushed her lips with a kiss, and he slipped past, refrigerator his destination.

Later that night, he was in bed with Kate, about to doze off, his back turned away from her and her insomnia. It was the same, night after night. She would not fall asleep and eventually, she said, she'd give up and leave bed to watch late-night TV.

"I'm afraid," she said, surprising him.

He rolled over. She had pulled the blanket to her chin, as if to keep some fear at bay. "I feel like something awful's gonna happen."

The words went through him. Was Kate going to let loose the accusations she really had on her mind when she caught him with his laptop full of Averyl?

Whatever, he kept quiet, not volunteering anything.

Kate, with wide, dread-filled eyes courtesy of Edvard Munch, seemed about to say something more.

He pulled her head closer.

"You might have to take me to the hospital," she said.

His arm went slack—it wasn't Averyl. But what was wrong with Kate?

Any first aid he knew, he left in Vietnam. Silent images of buddies, long past, streamed through his mind's eye and they had the same horror in their faces that Kate now showed.

Yeah, he'd seen it in 'Nam, especially one time Lindsley in camp was cleaning his M-16 right after a bout of gunplay with Charlie while on recon. Lindsley handled that M-16 like it was a live snake and broke down in an anxious funk. Shell shock.

Like then, he took Kate's wrist, checked for vitals. On cue, the training came back. Her pulse was hammering away like the Sixties drummer Ginger Baker in Cream.

"You got a fast pulse," he said, not wanting to alarm her. "Why don't we go downstairs, sit in the parlor, it's cooler. I'll get you some water."

Minutes later, Kate, thin blanket about her shoulders, sat with him on one side of the couch, a single streetlight, a few houses away, giving forth the only light to intrude upon the darkness of the parlor.

"I felt fragile, like I was doomed," she said, holding the water glass to her lips with a slight tremor.

She was so vulnerable, a victim, he guessed, of hormones run amok. He was ready to sit with her the whole night if that's what she needed.

"Oh, it's happening again. I feel awful."

His thumb searched her wrist for a pulse. Sure enough, her heart raced like that drummer cut loose again. "Just take one deep breath for me. Try." Kate's head pushed back on her shoulders and she did her best with a fitful intake of air. "There. Deep breath in. Deep breath out."

The pulse seemed to slow once more. "That bad feeling, it comes in waves, until it plays itself out," he said, remembering how he, too, had some anxiety rushes in 'Nam, especially the last months of his tour.

Sure enough, she seemed calmer, less agitated by the anxiety demons. He felt not talking was best at that particular moment, for Kate was looking pensively at her lap, reflecting, perhaps, on the pure fear her body was offering up on its own.

He let go of her wrist, startled by the wash of street light that now fell tentatively across her face. His hand reached to caress her forehead where her bangs stopped in a precise line, the only line visible in that faint light. For in the meager light there were no wrinkles in Kate's face, no inklings of crow's-feet at the corners of her eyes. No, nothing more than the contours of this smooth skin that he knew was a face returned from those days so many years ago, which now seemed like yesterday, when he first knew her.

His fingers thrilled to the touch of her forehead and bangs for he knew this was the same woman, ageless, he'd fallen in love with those twenty-five years ago. And he knew that in that moment, as her head rose and fell with a deep breath and the light changed its play slightly over her wondrous facial shape, that he was fully capable of falling in love with her again. Maybe Averyl was only a misdirection of his best impulse.

He brought her closer to him and to his amazement, he could not see better, nor see less perfection, for the light and darkness together removed all lines of age from Kate's face.

"I'm keeping you up all night," she said, the suffering absent from her voice.

Then he bent close to her lips.

"Oh, here's another one," she said alarmed.

He kissed her anyway.

LA MOSCA

Laura had what she'd just as soon call "the faints." Oh, at first, Dr. Koppel assured her people got dizzy, fainted for dozens of reasons, all mostly harmless. But Tuesday Koppel took a pen from her white-coat pocket, pointed to a Rorschach of shadowy grays on a light panel—supposedly Laura's brain—and said, "Problem's here." Laura knew that luminous hazelnut-sized defect was a time bomb.

She next heard, "Medical intervention can't do much." Understandably, she forgot the unwieldy Latinate phrase for why she had no more than eighteen months of active life left. A prescription in hand, nothing more than a palliative, really, Laura walked steadily out to the clinic parking lot, no wiser.

She had to keep about the day's business, she reasoned, so the dizziness would not get her. Small, quotidian purposes could help. She would stay standing, as she did now, Friday morning, behind a glassed-in walkway across one wall of a multilane garage bay under a ceiling studded with evacuation fans. She would give complete attention to her Tercel spinning front wheels, going nowhere on enormous steel rollers, a sensor attached to its tailpipe. She would wonder, Can this aged car pass? A fifteen-year-old car had to be a match for her sixty-seven years.

The blue-jumpsuited technician gunned the motor. The front wheels skittered sideways. A quick steering wheel tug, though, and the guy had the car again tracking true. Then elbow out the driver's window, he studied an orange line wriggling across a computer display. He revved it up again.

Someone else joined Laura. A suit-and-tie man, cell-phoning, who declared, above the din of her testing-abused Tercel and other vehicles in the bay, "I'm at DEQ getting tested." Laura figured his anthracite black BMW, next up, was a business lease: new enough to be an automatic pass.

The technician, out of the car, hit a floor lever. The rollers retracted. He yanked the sensor off the tailpipe. Back in the car, he drove smartly forward, the brake lights flicking at the far apron of the garage.

Laura fished out twenty-one dollars for the inspection fee and walked out to pay.

"No charge," the cashier said, seeing Laura's money. "Your car failed." The woman's face seemed genuinely disengaged about having bad news and waited for a computer printout.

"You can take this to a mechanic to work on your car. Okay?"

Laura took the free printout, ready to accept the car was getting old like her.

She got in the Tercel, moved the seat up. She shrugged, turned the ignition key. If the motor had to be replaced, maybe she could sell the car, take the bus. *That* was one long-term solution.

Back at the house, Laura had, as ever, many things to do. She couldn't be sure if teaching Speech and Drama to distraction-prone high-schoolers wasn't easier than retirement.

She rattled around in this Irvington bungalow, generously sized with five bedrooms, one of a kind said to be built for large Irish-Catholic families in the Twenties. The house was appreciated all the more when she was left with Cath, Rob, and little Petey to bring up, post-ex, so many years ago. She got the house from him, worth then about a tenth of what houses like it went for now. But it had to be kept up.

In the downstairs sunroom, Laura grabbed the phone, dialed a number in Healdsburg, California.

"Good afternoon. Dry Creek Meditation Center. How can I help you?" the unseen woman said, upbeat as only a Golden Stater could be.

"Yes, I was talking with a friend, she said you've one-week retreats people sign up for." On her own, Laura had tried to meditate. Nothing much came of it. She would doze off. Still, the art of meditation was a mystery for which she was determined to gain initiation.

Cath's friend loved this place in Northern California. An old farm converted to a retreat on Dry Creek Road in Healdsburg, nestled among some of the best vineyards in Sonoma County. Nora liked the open, unpretentious approach. Cath, who personally was into the Alexander Technique, joked it would be nice having a Plan B.

"That's right," the Meditation Center woman said. "We have one coming up next week. Let me—check. There're vacancies."

Laura said okay, gave her credit card info, billing address, and other details: She'd pass up the historic hotel on the square downtown, the Spartan sleeping facilities at the retreat would work. Then she hung up.

Now she had to call and buy the plane ticket. This close to departure, where was she going to get a deal? But did money matter anymore? Yes, it mattered. She had people to think about. Grandchildren.

What was she going to tell her family? Her back shivered at how they might react. Would they suffer more than her?

In her head, okay, she had but months to live. But her stomach, implacably nauseous, knew better: Acceptance was far off. Far off, as in she needed time.

Laura would hold back, not tell them. If she were to talk about it now, what could she say? That she was in shock, she was fearful, she felt her body, always healthy, had betrayed her? How she was to accept that life had rewarded the three decades devoted to teaching and raising kids with this retirement—two years' worth—and then told her, That's it. Time's up.

The mute phone made her sigh. Her life at that moment was a joke. A joke about the spin of Fortune's wheel. And she would have a whole week at the Dry Creek Meditation Center to reflect on that. She glanced at her scribbled notes, took the piece of paper, and got up.

She climbed the stairs to the second floor, to what used to be Rob's room before it became a depository for school paperwork. Forms like the twenty-point checklist (with room for comments) the class filled out when someone gave a speech. She had reams of that one stacked by the rolltop desk Rob bought at an antiques place in Sellwood, deeming it worthy of his old room.

She wheeled the squeaking, wooden chair back from the desk, sat down, and slid the rolltop open.

Among the heap of her checkbook, some unanswered correspondence, and statements from the credit union, the phone company, and others lay an old fountain pen.

The clip of the pen was a golden arrow. A diamond-shaped blue jewel was set between the arrow feathering, right above the *P* in PARKER spelled vertically down the shaft.

She hadn't used the pen for years. Then one day, Cath found it, asked where it came from. Laura guessed, with three kids, one might have played with it, broken it. But she couldn't ask: She, after all, had abandoned the pen.

Between her fingers, she rolled the fountain pen by its barrel, a fancy plastic of gold swirls interlaced with horizontal black stripes. She unscrewed the end cap, exposing the Parker Vacumatic spring-loaded plunger. When the pen worked, the plunger drew ink. What could be simpler? She pressed the stuck plunger—neglect alone had not fixed the pen.

She stood up from the desk, went for the window light to study the pen detailing. A step, two steps, and her thoughts turned sluggish. The pen slipped between her fingers, her legs buckled. Her arms swung out and her shoulder hit first, her head striking both shoulder and outstretched arm. She lay there for minutes, eyes glazed, not conscious of the fountain pen, the room, or the window light. Her heart beat furiously and through her dilated vessels pushed blood headward more easily than when she stood.

It might have been two minutes or less, but Laura came to, saw she was on the hard oak floor, yet her head didn't hurt. What was she doing? Musing on an old pen and memories. An old pen, like her, probably not fixable anymore. But the pen reminded her about those signature cards stashed in the rolltop.

Cath would sign one for the credit union. Cath, Rob, and Petey—all of them—had to sign joint custody signature cards. That way, they'd each get immediate access to their own CD with her, if, as her lawyer said, she predeceased them. No probate, no estate taxes, just clean transfers of her savings to the children.

Now where were those signature cards?

Sunday afternoons, Laura anticipated Rob driving up in his red Eclipse. For the last few minutes, Laura had been checking her front window. One thing about Rob, if he was to be by at four-thirty, you could set your watch at his driving up. This Sunday, Liam sat beside him too.

"So how have you been?" Rob said, hugging a sack of groceries, kneeing aside the screen door. Towheaded Liam scooted by. "Remember, I'm cooking tonight, Mom. My secret recipe for pasta primavera. Say, Liam, get back here." The nine-year-old had collapsed on the sofa as if he were home.

"Liam, get up, get these groceries in the kitchen, okay?"

Liam shot Rob a glance of incredulity, but sprang up and took the groceries, evidently understanding his choices to survive the next few hours. In the kitchen, Liam unpacked the sack, arranging everything on the counter, and before long, water hissing, was washing the vegetables.

"So, Mom, about a month ago, you mentioned those fainting spells, that you might see a doctor, you ever do that?"

Rob's vague look suggested he was only trying to start conversation.

"Oh, Rob, I saw the doctor about something else, didn't mention the faints because they went away." That easily Laura gave the lie to her entire rack of worry this last month. But misspeaking herself hurt doubly: for the truth *and* for the lie.

"Well, I didn't think it much, your mentioning it. Just this loose thought bouncing around, Mom said she's having fainting spells. Say, it's best they go away on their own. I'm glad to hear that." Rob patted the sofa back, as if confirming all was right in Mom's house.

"Hey, Liam, you finished up in there?" Rob eyed the industrious son, sinkbound. "Don't you be running up Grandma's water bill. Why don't you get out here? Show us some of your oratorical skills." Rob's gaze resettled on Laura. "He's gonna be Patrick Henry, a Revolutionary Heroes program at school."

Liam shuffled in the living room, dropped down on the couch next to his dad, and beamed.

"You're not doing Patrick Henry's famous speech?" Laura was astounded anyone in grammar school might attempt that.

Liam nodded.

"He walks around the house memorizing his lines out loud. I've memorized most of it too," Rob said.

"You ready?" Liam asked. Rob and Laura's smiles were enough. Liam leapt up, turned to the door, facing an imaginary audience. "Mr. President, it is natural to man to indulge in illusions of hope."

Laura reveled at how her grandson enunciated.

"Let us not, I beseech you, sir, deceive ourselves."

Laura noted that Rob, too, was rapt with attention to his son's words, his knowing gestures.

"They tell us, sir, that we are weak; unable to cope with so formidable an adversary. But when shall we be stronger?" His head tilted up, Liam's words were solemn, convincing. Laura was witnessing a miracle. Did this same grandson a few years before squirm in a crib, his pink face confused with the world about him? Yes, nine years ago—it seemed like yesterday. So much, lately, seemed like yesterday. Was her memory playing tricks?

But Liam was speaking. That was the thing now. His voice rose and both his hands shot out with the fervent plea: "Almighty God! I know not what course others might take, but as for me, give me liberty or give me death!"

Salty tears tracked Laura's face. Liam bowed. She took a soft, limp handkerchief and daubed at her eyes. Then she stood. She had to hug him. This was the best news she had had in months. Her own grandson made her proud and could, if he chose, easily follow her footsteps.

She reached for Liam and the slowdown in her thoughts surprised her, her head heavy and then her legs funny. They buckled and she fell.

Rob jumped out from the sofa, but not in time. "Liam, go get a glass of water and a dishcloth in the kitchen, right now."

Liam, confused to see this, at first froze, then dashed to the kitchen.

Rob held his mom's delicate head up a few inches in one hand, the other hand feeling for her pulse at the wrist. Liam noisily ran water in the kitchen. Rob's eyes looked over his mom's blouse, saw that it heaved up and down in shallow takes. Her pulse, a bit speeded up, was hard to find. But she would be okay.

Laura's eyelids parted. Her eyes steadied.

Rob grabbed the dishcloth from Liam, dipped it in the water. He folded and placed the towel on her forehead as if the wet coolness would calm and draw out whatever had gripped his mom to faint away.

"Here, leave this glass, go get another, she might want a drink."

Laura saw shock, worry in her son's eyes. "Don't try to talk," he said. "Just keep resting. You can sit up in a minute."

Rob kept a thumb to her slight wrist. Laura felt strength in the legs she knew could stand, but this was embarrassing.

Looking at Rob, she realized nobody could do a thing. If she told them, it would upset everyone and change nothing. No, she would keep it private. They'd imagine more suffering than was there. It was not that bad, really. Just these faints and then as Dr. Koppel speculated, maybe one fainting spell from which she would not get up. No, she would not tell Rob. No matter how much he asked.

"You feeling better?" he said.

"Oh, I'm coming around, thanks."

Laura tried sitting up. Rob took her hands, helped her to her feet. She trudged to the sofa and sat down. Liam had ready a glass of water.

"Grandma, are you okay? The way you fell looked kinda scary."

"The doctor can't say what it is. Comes and goes."

"You should go back and have more tests," Rob said. "This been happening lately?"

"No, can't even remember the last one." Laura winced: She'd again misled Rob and Liam.

She turned to her grandson, remembering his splendid acting got her up to embrace him before the faint. "Liam, you do have talent. That you do."

"It comes pretty naturally," he said.

"Like his grandma," Rob added.

They talked about Liam and his future acting career and Liam seemed to bask in the attention. Laura liked talking shop after being away from teaching.

"Mother," Rob said, when talk lulled. "Let me know if there is anything I can do for you. I still think you should see your doctor pronto. That was a quick fall you took and if it had been on a harder surface—" He wrinkled his forehead. "I don't know."

"Now, don't worry. I've got an appointment next month. But you really want to do something for me, I need you to come by the house next week, check things over. I'd ask Cath, but you know how distracted she gets."

"You're gone for how long?"

"Whole week, down to the Bay Area."

"Oh, this the meditation place?"

"One and the same."

"Great. So I'll swing by, maybe get my helper to come along." Rob glanced at his son. "You've soccer Wednesdays, don't you?"

"Thursdays, Dad. All summer long, remember?"

"Okay, we'll come Wednesday."

And that was that. Rob cooked the pasta garlicky and the two guests ate like they were starving. And within the hour, Rob and Liam were off. They left and feeling wholly well Laura took consolation at keeping her burden private.

The next day, Monday morning, Laura drove up Broadway to where Gary Nicklaw—a master mechanic for all Japanese cars—had a shop.

She parked and entered the window-free waiting room. Gary rested a phone on his shoulder, scribbled away at the counter. "Be with you in a minute," he whispered to Laura. She stood stiffly, elbows snug to her sides like someone with no idea how many dollars would make her car okay. In the claustrophobic room with one chair, she meditated on the few wall pictures: Gary with trophies beside some sports car. Gary looked a lot younger; the car, like a Japanese model no longer made.

Gary slipped the phone back in its cradle. "So, Ms. Grasmanis, note here says you didn't pass DEQ."

Laura opened her bag, took out the folded sheet with the pollution numbers.

Gary flattened the paper on the counter, sat chin in palm and took a deep breath. "So that's an eighty-five, isn't it? How many miles you got?"

"Oh, a hundred thousand, easily," Laura said, sure this meant the engine was kaput.

"You know, this being the first time you failed and a car that age, I bet we're talking bad catalytic converter."

"I didn't know I had one."

"Yeah, they're been on cars a while. Anyway, we'll check everything out, but that mileage, the engine's usually burning some oil." He drew a circle in the air with his pen. "And that gums up your converter—all this honeycomb inside, okay?" He held his hands apart, fingers spread. "Basically your converter's along for the ride—" He bounced his pen on the DEQ report. "And so, bad numbers."

When Gary said he'd remove and replace the converter for no more than one seventy-five, Laura felt a calm change her. The car, its smog test was the one thing on her to-do list she had to take care of before the registration deadline in two weeks. Now she could. She'd go to California with that lined out. She gave Gary the car key, the phone number to reach her, and then crossed Broadway. When the Tri-Met bus came, her spirit was as content as the camel that found the oasis well.

Thursday, before noon, Laura left home in the DEQ-legal Tercel and hopped on the Banfield Freeway, eastbound, for the Portland Airport. She had plenty of time to park long-term and catch her flight to San Francisco.

The idea of one whole week at Dry Creek Meditation Center let her ignore that she was poking along behind a semitrailer truck. It didn't bother her at all. She'd be in the bucolic wonderland of Sonoma County soon enough.

Then the huge truck shuddered with a noisy downshift that jetted black smoke skyward.

Laura braked. The slowing truck was signaling right, moving off at the 68th Avenue exit. A clear stretch of slow lane opened up.

She peered through the clean windshield. She'd had the car washed only yesterday, forgetting, for a week, it would sit outside. Better if she washed it when she got back. Oh, well, she could do that too. She dropped the worry for the sky was as blue as ever and a brilliant sun lazed in the south.

The world had awoke fresh. Just like the day, ten or more years ago, when those building climbers came to Portland from Bolivia. It was the craziest thing. Something like 35,000 people turned out on a Sunday afternoon, with summer weather exactly like it was today.

Las Moscas Humanas, The Human Flies, were about to climb—without ropes and without safety nets—the forty-two stories of Big Pink. The glass skyscraper on Fifth had been nicknamed for its flamboyant hue. A CNN satellite-dish truck broadcast live. Nothing this big had hit Portland since Mount St. Helen's blew in 1980, covering the town with powdery ash.

Laura and thousands of others crowded in the blocked-off streets. Before the climb, people listened to radio and TV broadcasts. She never knew so many people had portable TVs.

"This is a once-in-a-lifetime, I'm sure," said the announcer on the radio in the hand of a gray-haired, pony-tailed man next to her.

Laura craned her neck above the horizon of heads to the bank tower. Already on the second floor, on the glassy expanse, four men were moving, ascending in a diamond pattern. They wore identical red and blue and yellow silky robes, aflutter with the breeze and the upward hikes of one limb at a time.

"On their hands, The Human Flies have special polymer suction devices. Tremendous holding power," the radio announcer said. "That's how they can risk their lives. And their tennis shoes, custom-manufactured, have got dozens of small suction cups."

Laura squinted. Why would anybody do this? The precise diamond pattern *Las Moscas* kept on the pink glass must have inviolably attached them to the sheer side of the glass monolith. Laura had to believe that. But her back thrilled with fear.

Now to the tenth floor, their apparent size rendered them insects. Shrinking minute by minute, they seemed ultralight and the waving red, blue, and yellow robes, wings that might fly them to the top.

The Human Flies kept on the move in a strict sequence. Each moved in turn, left hand pneumatically clamping the glass with suction, then right hand, then each foot. Then another did the same. Agape, she could barely breathe and her mouth had gone dry.

The same motions over and over. Then time stopped. Laura's craning neck had froze. Hypnotized, she had followed *Las Moscas* past the halfway point, a fact the radio announcer exclaimed. They'd advanced to the twenty-second floor.

Then, suddenly, a loud gasp came from so many in the crowd. One figure was silently dropping away from the diamond—red, blue, and yellow robes fluttering to no effect. Like a released anchor, he was plummeting past every floor that *Las Moscas* had laboriously climbed.

He fell and fell, did not cry out. Laura squinted to see this brave man, for the first time facing her and the crowd, live his last moment. She had no choice. She couldn't look away, even if she wanted to go some place and lie down and be sick. And she saw that, in multicolored silky splendor, the young man had joined his arms and hands overhead. And amazingly, pointed his toes.

Those seconds of grace Laura never, ever, would get out of her mind.

Laura was approaching the 205 Interchange and the memory of that fallen daredevil, oddly enough, energized her. She signaled to go right. And, abruptly, her thoughts seemed sluggish.

Everything—the blue sky above, the summer light, the windshield—dimmed for Laura.

Within minutes, traffic on the Banfield was stop-and-go. Officer Gus Carrola had arrived on the scene in a black Camaro with doors emblazoned OREGON STATE POLICE. On the car roof, what the troopers called Christmas tree lights winked away. A fellow from a pickup rig, parked on the shoulder, had walked back and told Carrola he didn't know what happened.

The woman in the Tercel was driving along in the slow lane, where he was stuck two cars back, when all of a sudden tires squeal, the car shoots right and off the road. It takes out shrubbery. It hooks around. It pinballs across three lanes of freeway. It misses passing cars. It hits the freeway divider head-on. Then its rear wheels bounce up once.

"Was like nobody driving that car," the witness with the John Deere cap said. His eyes darted back to the Tercel nosed into the divider, hood buckled like a crushed pop can, a small figure inside slumped forward.

A hundred yards or so ahead, the green-and-white overhead freeway sign read, EXIT 8, 205 NORTH, SEATTLE, PORTLAND AIRPORT. Officer Carrola keyed into a dashboard-mount laptop the plate number for the Tercel across the way. His other hand held a mike. He was waiting for Emergency Dispatch to call back. Then he'd get the flares out of the trunk. He'd have in thirty years coming up in October. Retirement had to be easier than this.

TALKING CABBAGE HEADS

What's my game? Here you go, a few clues: Bok choy. Carrots, tops, no tops. Radicchio. Lettuces. Hey, lettuces I got. Crispy iceberg. Chewy romaine. Spunky Bibb. Something more Continental? What do you say to an *insalata mista* of tossed greens: endive, dandelion, escarole, arugula? Okay, time's up, you Sherlock.

You probably walked around me, my cart full of cabbage heads. That is, if you shop here at Planet Foods, so now's good as time as any for introductions. Austin, call me Austin. I'm your basic twenty-year-old American male, originally from Eugene, now resident up here in Portland because a produce driver I know through my dad thought Planet Foods was hiring.

Six months ago, I decided no college for me. Thought about AmeriCorps briefly. Very briefly, like, okay, I was reaching for something. I kinda felt I had to make changes in my life. Get away from Eugene and Dad's tiresome dirt farming—eight acres in corn, a back-to-the-land leftover from the Seventies, he and Mom were into about the time I was born.

Anywho, this working dayshift in produce fit my plan to, one day, get the scoop on what all my life could be. First thing I did, though, I get to Portland, was change my name.

Got tired of being called Ocean, my birth name. That is so Seventies. It's like disco-dead and buried. So I told them here,

"Make the checks out to Austin." Great name, Austin, sounds enough like Ocean, it's only this partial identity change, see?

"Excuse me," this thin woman, fortyish and attractive, says. Her black hair's one of those Yuppie cuts probably costs more than I make in a week.

She dislodges one of the romaines in the bin that's half-empty, asks if I'll check in back for some that's fresher. You know, a customer like this thinks for her business we'll do cartwheels. I'm about to unstack, then restack six, ten heavy boxes? Please, don't get me started.

"Hmmm. New delivery's in an hour," I lie. "You check back then, I'll have out the new romaine."

The woman thanks me. Makes me feel like such a loser, this misleading her. I mean, what delivery? The romaine I'll put out, I'm putting out later because that's when I get to what we got in back.

Other than my small deception, this foxy woman must have it made. She's angling her cart to the apples, oranges. Husband, I bet, has a good job. She doesn't work, cruises in and out of here, shops at her leisure. What she's gotta do? Keep that figure, get in an aerobics class few times a week, stay in shape. Then cross her fingers the old man doesn't go with any wayward urges. All the time, seems to happen.

Like I was saying, I change my name to Austin, my dad he comes around, accepts it. Jokes about it at first, natch. But my mom, forget it. She'll never stop calling me Ocean, says that's one change she can't handle. It's not me if I'm not Ocean, she says. Oh, sure, like me and Dad few years back had to accept that she'd met the "love of her life" when she decides to move out, live with this lounge lizard across the river in Springfield. I tell you, more those wayward urges.

Whoa, it's already 10:30. Breaktime. I live for morning breaks.

"So what's new with you, your girlfriend in Eugene?" Brianna from deli asks. She's joined me on break.

"Calls, says she's just back from Phoenix, gonna start community college there."

"Arizona?"

"Yeah. At first I thought that Phoenix down by Medford."

"Why'd she go out of state?"

"Probably same reason I'm here: Gotta try living away from home. And she says the weather."

"And you?"

"She didn't say."

Where was I? Hmmm. These icebergs. Gotta rotate. See, pull what's here in the bin. Check 'em out. Whip off those leaves going bad.

Okay, now the rebuild. New heads in back. Listen up, friend, this is your produce tip for the day: Go back, go down, that's the good stuff. Don't be afraid to dig it out if you gotta. There now the old stuff goes on top.

So anyway I'm talking to Dad about Kim, her Phoenix surprise. He goes to recycling his idea at me I should be in community college too. Which I understand. He teaches at Lane Community. You might say it's his real job to support that corn acreage.

But it's the same-old-same-old talk. Like six months ago, I told him the last thing I wanted to do was go off to college *undecided*. Undecided is a fat waste, time and money.

At least I'm here. I could see, if it wasn't college, Dad snaring me into some endless hours of farm chores—let me be honest, disked dirt doesn't make my heart thump. Which is why I thought it best to get out of Eugene, get a job, and buy some time and space to think.

So now Kim's done given me the slip. Fine. Neither one of us is gonna be around Eugene much anyhow.

There those are up. Let me show you the backroom.

Here's Operations Central: We pull deliveries, organize boxes, get it all ready to take out and stock. See that chunker on the dock over there? He's Dennison. Bossman. He looks this way.

"Austin."

"I'm listening."

"Get together with Todd before you take off 'bout bailing cardboard. I'm tired of seeing it lying around in the morning."

"Yep, it's gotta be bail early, bail often."

"Another thing, he's tells me more than once you've left all the boxes for him to do—I don't know who of you's flaking—so you two work it out, okay?"

"Whatever it takes."

That Dennison's prime, isn't he? Likes to play Todd and me off against each other. Basic move from his jerkmeister manual.

Sometimes I just gotta put the distance between us. Which is why I grabbed these boxes of eggplant, threw 'em on the cart, and removed my person from that backroom.

I tell you, I feel at times like that whole salmon on ice over there in the deli case. Poor fish ever get what he was born for? Not in this go-round.

The Northwest used to be great salmon country. Salmon had run of the rivers. Made for one of nature's beautiful cycles. Now it's all completely corrupted. Originally, you know, salmon came down the Columbia River and were in the Pacific Ocean in one week. Now, thanks to the dams, how about six weeks? Okay, they're endangered. Guess what that means? The politicians, in deep dough-dough, play badminton, until none are left.

I tell you what needs doing. I organize a Salmon Liberation Front, we commandeer a Cessna east of here, we fly up the Columbia Gorge, we enter the airspace right over Bonneville and then, doors open, shove, push, out goes your basic A-bomb to the target below and hope to hell that Cessna would hold together once the Mother of All 'Shrooms comes up to greet us.

Haven't got the personal survival part down, but I'm working on it. Maybe it's woolgathering to pass the time while I get these eggplants replaced. Doesn't hurt, though. I figure out how to save the salmon, we all might make it on this planet. What comes 'round, goes 'round. I gotta believe that.

"Say, you throwing that eggplant out? I wanted to buy some." It's one of our regular customers, *always* in torn Levi's.

"Not to worry, mon," I say, unsure if he'll loosen his attitude. "I'm just culling what hasn't sold."

"Wow, that seems a waste. One soft spot and—" Like an umpire, his thumb's past the stringy blond hair and he flashes me a needling grin. "Ever think about marking this down, putting it on sale?"

Why, of course. I'm thinking heaps of bananas gone black, buzzing fruit flies—all this at Planet Foods?! "Hmmm. Store image would be hurtin' we do that, the store owners want fresh, fresh, fresh," I say, reluctant about getting into it with him.

"So that eggplant—" He points at what I've got. "You're saying I can't buy it full price and gotta wait, get it for free in the garbage?"

These culls are soft, no taut purply skins like on what's below, unopened, in the boxes this guy hasn't noticed. I see the guy's buttons—figure of speech—get his act right away. He probably shops here 'cause so much of our stuff's organic. On food matters, he's gotta be one elitist in torn Levi's. I mean, pesticides terrify him. Like he hit a patch of financial embarrassment, he'd settle for pulling our organic oranges, our organic cabbages out of the Dumpster. He'd tell himself by eating garbage he was extending the world food supply, letting starving people eat. Just gotta save that world. Could be he's a bit like me, my Cessna fixing to free the salmon. I just nod and grin, and ask him, "You eat a lot of produce?"

"I'm a vegetarian."

"Figures. Here tell you what, let's get a boxboy-size bag. I'll give you all the bruised and dented stuff you want, nickel a pound, whatta you say?"

"You can do that?"

"Watch this."

I take my handy-dandy grease pencil from my apron pocket and for checkout write on the bag, "SURPLUS @ 5¢/LB SKU 9999," and initial it. Dennison has a mind to crucify me, selling what we throw out, I'll let everyone know. Razzing him would put my interest in this job at high tide for weeks.

"Say, dude, you should run this place."

"Not just yet," I say. I know when to move on's gotta come in its own sweet time.

I snap open that big brown kraft bag so we can start shopping for what's ripe, bad, and ugly. Veg-Man's eyes widen—he's ready to gather in the cornucopia. "You big on romaine lettuce?" I ask, getting things underway.

PAST PERFECT

Friday, at seven in the morning, Kyla, dressed in civvies—jeans and a RACE FOR THE CURE T-shirt—took husband Paul to PDX. He was outbound for an eight-day business trip. While he could have, that early, managed a cab, she volunteered. They hadn't had time, with the press of their jobs (he, a software engineer for Cirrus; she, HomeFinder Realty's top producer) to hash over what their son, Alex, had in the way of plans, or lack thereof, for the summer when he came back from U of O later that day.

  Five hours after she hugged, kissed Paul good-bye at the Southwest gate for Albuquerque, Kyla told sixteen-year-old daughter Zoe, achingly thin like all her girlfriends, that she was gone to get Alex. She took Steve's cavernous Tahoe and drove the 110 miles from their Irvington Tudor to the yellow-striped loading zone in the shadow of a towering concrete dormitory on a May afternoon in Eugene under a blue, windless sky.

  Kyla had cell-phoned Alex thirty minutes out of Eugene. Just now, he rushed down the sidewalk, blond buzz cut, shabby jeans, easily the winner of any moving-day-casual contest with Mom.

  "Wow, am I glad you're here. I brought everything down the freight elevator and it's all in the lobby, as we speak now."

  Kyla hugged Alex, felt almost teary at how much taller he was than she. It had not been that many years since the growth spurt. "So how did the final go?" She had cut out the phone calls after Alex's machine message proclaimed him in marathon study sessions for the biology exam the day before.

"Oh, okay. It was all multiple-choice and I never have a clue how I did with *those*."

"I'm sure you did fine. Say, we can get it all in here, don't you think?" Kyla eyed the garage-sized maw of the Tahoe, rear door open.

"Sure, why don't we lay the bike down sideways and put the garment bags, everything else on top?"

They ferried the moving cart from the dorm a few times. Then with Alex's accumulated belongings from one year at U of O on board, Kyla closed the door. "That's that."

"Be back, *un secondo*," Alex said, playfully pushing the cart up the sidewalk to the dorm, in what seemed an expression of carefree relief that he was going home.

S aturday morning, Kyla was up early. Alex was home again. She had a full day of houses to show and one couple was ready to buy.

Kyla cooked eggs and bacon and a sluggish Alex, wearing an old bathrobe, padded in, yawning.

"Where's Zoe?" she asked.

"Party girl, sleeps in."

"Then it's the two of us." She smiled—it really was her firstborn home again. "Here, all your favorites."

"Oh, Mother, you didn't have to—"

"Let's eat, I have to leave in fifteen minutes."

"And bacon! I told you I'm a vegetarian, didn't I?"

She sipped her coffee, ignoring him. Alex had been a picky eater all his life.

"I'm sorry, meat is so gross."

Her eyes flared wide. She did a mental ten-count and kept eating.

Alex fussed with toast and butter and after the awkward silence, Kyla pursued idle chitchat—How'd you sleep? Like this break from studying? Then she left.

The rest of the day was all good news. Namely, an earnest money note a couple with a three-year-old boy in tow signed.

With such an embrace of good fortune, Kyla returned home and found Alex and Zoe in back. Alex slumped in an Adirondack chair, a vegetarian Diet Coke in hand. Zoe, on the porch with CD caliper earphones horseshoeing her neck.

Alex placed the can on the broad chair arm. "I tell you guys, Chase and I celebrated our six-month anniversary before I left?"

"Yeah, Chase, dreadlocks," Kyla said, remembering a disheveled character from a hurried visit to Eugene months before. "Anniversary of *what*?"

"Sex—what else?"

Zoe tittered. Alex grinned with obvious satisfaction.

"I'm concerned about you, Alex. I hope you're keeping your priorities—uh—in mind."

"I can't even think straight anymore. Ha, ha." Alex drank more Coke and seemed to delight in Kyla's awkward sensitivity. "Let's not slide into homophobia, Mom."

Zoe slipped on the earphones and pressed PLAY on the Sony—she knew well this argument—and seemed ready to open the screen door and go in the house.

Kyla gave Zoe no attention and ignored Alex's victimhood baiting. "Priorities, Alex. Priorities, two thousand a month keeps you in Eugene. So don't joke around. We just don't want to see you throw everything away."

Kyla studied Alex, looking for assent. She didn't see any. All she saw was the characteristic squinch in Alex's face, a telltale sign from almost toddler days that Alex was stuck in thought, couldn't decide what to say.

"We don't care what you study," Kyla continued. "We only want you to give yourself a future."

Alex started humming Elgar's "Pomp and Circumstance." He smirked, screwing up his face in silliness.

Zoe stopped her CD and bent forward. "Sorry. I'd like to stay, but, Mom, I gotta get going, I have to be at Cydney's tonight, remember? I have to get ready."

"Okay, have a good time," Kyla said as if she had heard the plan before.

The screen door spring creaked and Zoe left. Kyla restudied Alex. "I'm serious about this," she said.

"Sure, like that valedictorian bit, Give yo'self a future. People have been giving and giving me advice all my life."

"I told you, Alex, major in anything you want."

"But this pressure's crazy. Thousands and thousands of dollars, wrap up that education, young man," he said, doing his best to fake a basso profundo. "You've got thirty-six months."

Kyla looked away from Alex, as if she'd let him get over his peevish outburst.

"The way you guys talk," he continued in a soft voice, "it's like paying off some car loan. I need a timeout."

Alex was going to sit around the house apparently all summer and do nothing. He had no plans. She stared at him in disbelief and gaped at what illogic possessed him. "This is your break. Three months off, right now. What's up with you?"

"I was thinking maybe in fall instead of starting classes, I'd do something different."

"What? Stay here?"

"No, Chase was talking, we'd go off to Europe for six months. It's a good time to travel through France, Italy—the summer tourists are gone."

"Okay, I'll level with you," she said steepling her fingers, gazing at Alex. "I'm a bit put out. And if Paul were here, I'd bet he'd say the same things, only more so. We wouldn't work as hard, schlepping around, if it weren't for you and Zoe and what you two might make of yourself with the right opportunities."

"But I want to be with Chase," he said softly.

"Not good enough. This sounds like you're quitting on school. What are you doing for money? Give that any thought?"

"Gee, always comes back to money, doesn't it? Don't worry, Chase's parents aren't strapped for cash." His face, mercurial as ever, switched from vulnerable to smirky.

"Don't think Chase's parents might not hear from us."

Alex glowered.

"Paul is not going to like this," she said.

"That's new?" He eyed what was left in the Coke can and then gave it a bottom's-up swallow.

"Listen, I won't mention it when he calls tonight. You'll have time to think it over before he gets back."

"So will you. You two better find some acceptance on this one." On the chair arm, Alex placed the Coke can on its side and with the edge of his palm crushed it to a *U*.

The rest of that evening they did not talk.

When Alex went to bed that night, he told her, in a voice of exhausted feeling, he would like to sleep in tomorrow morning. Kyla, sipping Scotch, did not take her eyes off Letterman and said, "Okay."

The Sunday morning routine was a refuge from the fallout of arguing with Alex. Kyla was up brewing coffee, snagging a weighty *Oregonian* off the mossy concrete front steps before eight. She hugged what felt like pounds of newsprint, sleeved in thin plastic, tied off at one end. While newspapers had to be dry, she hated figuring out how to extricate the jumble of daily tidings from its protective film. Paul always did that.

In the kitchen, she yanked open a drawer, rooted about for scissors among the miscellany of utensils. No scissors. A small chef's knife caught her eye. That had to do.

Drawer pushed in, cutting board out, stroking the knife edge across the butt end of the sleeved newspaper, a few disconnected cut marks. Did Paul ever sharpen knives?

The knife handle regripped, a stab downward, a pull backward, an opening in the plastic. Knife on the counter, clinched teeth, both hands in the opened plastic. The knife again, sawing at the opening. Success. The film came off.

She took the paper to the deck in back, where her coffee had gone tepid in the morning air. She fumbled the paper off the table and trudged back inside to microwave the coffee.

Already it was eight-fifteen. When Alex said he would sleep in, What did that self-righteous twit mean? Noon?

The microwave beeped. Kyla took the coffee and returned to mound the newspaper spillings on the deck table.

She turned automatically to the home listings, then fished out the *Living* section for her horoscope, but read nothing about what she was going through.

She did not look forward to telling Paul about Alex. He would warm up to the idea of Alex leaving school to travel with Chase no quicker than an iceberg. Just when they thought they had brought Alex along through eighteen long years, readied him to be a successful adult, this had to happen. The rocket blows up on the launchpad.

Kyla flipped through the paper, section by section, reading nothing. Her head ached. She was thinking about Paul, Friday back from Albuquerque, he would submarine into a prolonged sulk about Alex. Not talking, not helping her. Between Alex and Paul, Kyla saw weeks looming of insufferable family tension. She sighed and stood up to return to the kitchen for more coffee.

Upstairs, noises came from Alex's room. Alex could be a light sleeper, but those heavy thumps? She left the coffee cup on the counter to check.

On the second floor, at the end of the hall, Alex's door was slightly ajar. Odd because Alex always kept the door closed when he was sleeping, did so ever since he was a child. Kyla took that portal gap as an invitation.

"Alex, you're not awake, are you?" Kyla asked not out of courtesy, but as a gambit to see what was going on. Obviously, all that motion was not sleeping.

"I'm busy," Alex said in a huff.

That two-inch gap of room view disappeared with a door slam.

It was Kyla's house, after all, and her son's privacy be damned, she was not about to back down from a door shut in her face. She stepped closer, had her hand on the door knob, but did not turn it.

"Alex, I don't want to start where we left off last night."

No response from the other side, just more tossing things around.

Kyla had not the faintest what Alex might be doing. "But you are going to have to sit down with Paul and me and discuss with us calmly and rationally what you're going to do about college."

Silence.

Then slapping sounds and steps and *whoosh*, the door opened, revealing Alex, holding soft luggage that bulged like beach balls.

"This isn't working, I'm leaving."

Kyla was paralyzed. Her son staring her down like she was a stranger, like he was nothing more than an overnight guest ready to resume travel.

"Just like that," she managed to say, her throat feeling dry. "Can't you stick around to see your father?"

"I'll call him when he's back." Alex sighed as if he were Atlas. "I hardly slept last night, I'm ready to leave." He hiked up the luggage like a march down the stairs would get him out that front door.

"If you're going back to Eugene, I can give you a ride."

"Thanks, but I'll use your phone and cab it to the Greyhound station."

With an intuitive sense her son was leaving the nest for good, Kyla reached for one of the bags and together they shuffled out the hallway, down the steps, across the landing, down the steps, and over the entryway to the sunroom where Alex phoned.

"The cab'll be here in fifteen minutes," he said. "That gives us some time to talk." Alex had that annoying smirk on his face.

With an index finger, Kyla gently wicked away at her eyes what might have soon been tears. She wanted to tell Alex that they, the family, would always be there for him. That this was his home. But that smirk, which probably Alex could not help, meant she could not say anything that was in her heart.

"I was just thinking," she said. "If you'd known you were going to cause all this confusion, it might have been better if you stayed in Eugene with Chase."

They both laughed. Kyla hugged her son like it had to be for the last time.

CYDNEY'S BENT

These days, Cydney doesn't look like she fell in the tackle box. Piercings are out. Her right nostril lost a gold ring. The other nostril heals the puncture where a faux emerald stud stuck. And the ears that were laddered with six delicate hoops each: no metal there. And *pièce de résistance*, Cydney's left eyebrow hoop, too rad, gone.

A hoop for her lower lip was next, when she noticed that *that look*, especially among the other sophomores at Markham was like so *everywhere*. It was time to move, time to go different.

The mirror in Cydney's room tells no lies: The new look is, way cool. This afternoon, her hair was layer-cut two inches long, all over. After the cutting, after the color-stripping, her first dye job: Flamingo Pink. Cydney scopes it out. She could almost hug herself. Her truly cotton candy hair's gotta stand out from all those pop-top people walking around school.

But she has to wait 'til Monday. It's Friday night and nothing better's doing than getting online, seeing if Zoe's chatting. Zoe's three blocks away, in Irvington too.

>*Cydney89: i got 107 mp3s of possum.*
>*zoewhat: no way, girl. they record that much???*
>*cydney89: lot o' versions. like i got 5 thunder woman. concerts, all different cities.*
>*zoewhat: you need a player, a rio.*
>*cydney89: no, i need a minidisc, but they're expensiv-o.*

zoewhat: how much?

cydney89: $350. dad's refused already.

zoewhat: can you save your allowance? (smiles.)

cydney89: oh, sure, i'm thinking with bus passes and all, i live on water, i could buy one, maybe 6 months.

zoewhat: no minidisc 4 u. (smiles.)

cydney89: wrong. i'm going 4 a job tomorrow. got 2 make money.

Next day, Cydney's at Boss Burger on Broadway, lunchtime people packing the place. Some Markham kids too. They double take and Cydney knows: Flamingo Pink rocks. Yet, despite the attention, she's got the willies.

She wants to leave immediately. She's never filled out a job application. And she hates the idea, even with cool hair: REJECTION stamped on the Boss Burger Application for Employment she still has to fill out.

Jason's the tall and lanky manager. He takes Cydney's application and bugs someone to get over to condiments. Cydney follows Jason to a two-seat table in back.

"Give me a min," he says, moving his finger across the application. Cydney swears this Jason guy's lips move on some words he reads.

He flips the sheet over, evidently checking she's signed and dated.

He takes the app by a corner, waves it over like he'll read through again, then says, head down, "This your first job?"

She still has the willies. Leaving out the Christmas tree lot last year—though she got rooked out of any pay—was a mistake. "Yes, my first *real* job. I've done baby-sitting, off and on, for neighbors." Of course, Cydney's never baby-sat in her life.

Jason seems okay with that and her legs now don't feel so knotted up, like she wants out immediately. He keeps studying the app that took her sixty seconds, tops, to fill out. She bites her lip. What if he says no? Boss Burger is, well, *so boss*.

"Okay, tell you what, this reference, Ms. Kawabata—" He says the name slowly like it's a syllabic trap. "She your teacher at Markham?"

"Yes."

"Good, let you know, anyone we hire, we check references. I'll do it later. Right now I need someone else working the till swing-shift, starting at four."

Cydney gapes. Is she hired? Boom! Like that?!

"We bring you on board, you understand, this Ms. Cowabunga," he says, rushing the name now, "she's gotta tell me you're responsible, okay?"

Cydney nods.

"Let me tell you about the job."

Jason begins a recitation of what meal-order takers at Boss Burger do. He says all this like dozens of minimum-wagers before Cydney helped him commit it to memory. He tells Cydney it's orders both at the counter and the drive-up window. She takes money, she makes change, and she posts orders, all from the electronic register. She doesn't cook food. She gives food to customers and, for that and other reasons, she strictly observes the State of Oregon hygienic standards for food handlers. At all times, she wears a paper Boss Burger cap, covering her hair. Jason says this without so much as a smile. Then, he winds up by saying tomorrow she trains with Marin.

Cydney leaves Boss Burger, now positive the MiniDisc is but weeks away. Traffic on Broadway rushes by and in her oh-so-small purse she reaches for the oh-so-small cell phone. Flips it open to speed-dial Mom with the news, except getting this job at Boss Burger was too easy. Although she's pumped about getting the MiniDisc, what work was it to get hired? She sat there and that Jason guy didn't even look her in the eye. She was the warm body. She snaps the cell phone shut.

Sunday afternoon, Cydney shows up at Boss Burger, finds an empty locker in the employee room, puts away her purse, her fleece anorak. She snaps open a Boss Burger paper cap, tugs it on.

A mirror hangs opposite the lockers. She checks her look once more.

The face in the mirror says, *Ridiculous*. Her head, well-shaped, topped off with short Flamingo Pink locks, now seems unbalanced with this disposable paper cap. She slips a finger under the edge of the paper cap to coax out more flashy strands. So she can be more Cydney, even in a silly cap. She sighs. She's ready for hungry, noisy mobs when through the window of the swinging door, she sees Jason comes this way.

He stands there, holding the door open and checks her out, it seems. Cydney bites her lip. What's with this guy? Couldn't bother to look me in the eye when he hired me.

He smiles or maybe it's something like a sneer. She wants him out of the way, so she can get with Marin and get training. But he's boss.

"Too bad the cap covers your hair," he says. He could almost be nice, except Cydney has no idea where this guy is coming from. No idea.

"I'll live," she says.

"You been jello-fighting?"

She says nothing.

Jason looks like a comedian who misfired a joke. "Not funny, okay. Say, Marin's not here. You got a cap, here's a badge. Let's go talk about the till."

Marin clocks in thirty minutes late and Cydney's glad to finally see her. She's decided Jason, who she guesses is in his thirties, if not forties, is all he'll ever be, being this Boss Burger manager. And that fact, in a way, bums her like Marin doesn't.

Marin's seventeen, went to Grant, and only works for the extra cash. She dresses like she's already at UC Santa Cruz: stonewashed jeans and a Powell's tee. Marin tells Cydney her hair is stylin'. Cydney is ready to learn the job.

Two hours later, they break for dinner. After today, Cydney better be a self-starter, so she gives Marin complete attention for the details about how employees do meals. You can bring your own food, put it in the fridge, and later microwave. But you can't sit in the public area with your own food. Or Boss Burger lets you eat anything from the menu at half-price and deducts from your next paycheck. You don't even need cash. Most employees, Marin says, eat Boss Burger.

Today, Cydney goes for the chicken sand. Marin, the chef's salad. Marin's talked for most of the last two hours and understandably goes quiet once she starts forking into the lettuce.

"I can't wait to get out of this place in August," Marin says finally.

Cydney is unsure what *that* means. "What are you really anxious to go to college?" she says, trying to stay neutral.

"No, college will be hard enough. It's this working with customers." She holds her clear plastic fork up like she's about to kabob a customer or two on tines. "If I never, ever, hear whining again about too much mayo or too little mustard, I'll know God exists. That would prove for me she exists." Marin throws her head back and gives Cydney a sidelong glance, like she's the one getting out of the fast food business and Cydney's the one getting in.

"Well, I don't plan to do this forever. I want to get funds for a MiniDisc, that's my plan, sorta."

"That's cool. Anyway, like I was saying we take thirty minutes on this break, then we do drive-up window, okay?"

"Welcome to Boss Burger. What would you like to order?" Cydney says this, laughing. She already knows that much.

The next day, Monday night, Cydney's live at the drive-up window. It's like working walkups inside. Register's the same, menu's the same, though everything's packed to go. A monitor overhead shows where orders are. She's bends her head back so much, she's sure it was designed for someone taller, say Shaquille O'Neal, he ever decided to take more modest pay and work at Boss Burger.

"Good evening, welcome to Boss Burger. May I take your order?"

"How much is water?" this voice barks in Cydney's headset.

"Water's free. How many cups you want?"

"One water. And make it small." The headset hisses, then, "Tiffany, you gotta to go yet?" Then, "Make it a small water."

"Anything else?" Cydney says, thinking, if not, this is one silly order and one silly reason to wait in a drive-up window line.

"Yes, three Deluxes, okay?" Before Cydney hits Boss Burger Deluxe three times on the keyboard, the voice booms back. "One Deluxe gots light on lettuce, no pickles, lots of mustard and lots of mayo."

Cydney searches for pencil and paper. Marin didn't mention custom burgers. She bites her lip. What gives? And the keyboard's got no button like HOLD PICKLES, no way.

"Then one everything 'cept no tomato, extra bacon." A pause. "Tiffany, you say you gotta to go bad? Make up your mind." More air of headset hiss, then, "Where was I? Yeah, extra bacon. Got that?"

Cydney has no idea where this order, these changes, are going. None of it's on the keyboard, except for water and the Deluxes.

She should call Jason to set it straight, but she doesn't see him around. She should just deal with it, prove to herself she can handle the job.

"Okay, three Deluxes, one water. You want fries with that?"

"Whadya mean? I haven't even told you all that's in the last burger."

"We don't make custom burgers," Cydney says. "All Deluxes have two patties, lettuce, mayonnaise, mustard, pickles, bacon strips."

"Will you just wait, I always order burgers this way. Why don't you lissen?" the voice growls.

Someone in the drive-up line honks a horn. Cydney needs to finish this order.

"Tell you one more time, you get it right. One light on lettuce, no pickles, lots mustard, lots mayo. One no tomato, extra bacon. One regular. Got that? Why don't you repeat it?" This person has a mad-on that Cydney thinks funny because *she's* staying cool.

"It's okay, I heard you fine." Cydney could chuckle because the three Deluxes she keyed in *ages* ago are up, in a paper bag right next to her. "You want fries with that or not? What about drinks?"

A car honks again.

"Three large fries, one large Coke, one small Coke, one small water."

Cydney turns, drops three fries in the paper bag and gets going two Cokes at the dispenser. She keys in the rest of the order. "Ten seventy-five. Drive up to the first window, please."

Cydney closes her eyes. Then a rackety car, a woman's outside the window, glowering. Wiry in a housedress, she holds out a ten and a one, the other hand snubs a cigarette in the ashtray. Two small kids slither up and over the front seat.

She stares at Cydney, then takes back the money. "Let me see the hamburgers, see if you got it right."

"You gotta pay first, ma'am," Cydney says, reaching out for the money.

"You have so much trouble with the order, I thought I'm talking to a retard."

Cydney guesses the woman is nuts. "Ma'am, pay then you get the food."

"I thought I'm talking to a retard, now I know I'm talking to a retard, a pink-haired retard." The woman's smug-faced, like she's got the upper hand now. "Let me see the burgers."

Cydney's right hand, palm up and out for the money, transforms. She peels a banana for the woman and the two inattentive youngsters' private viewing pleasure. Shock wracks the woman's face, a sight that Cydney does not enjoy, she is so mad at having to take this abuse. The peeled banana, Cydney's middle finger soloing, points right at the woman's tobacco-stained teeth that will not be eating any Deluxe Boss Burger this evening. Cydney has shown this nuts-o woman the score.

"I wanna talk to the manager," the woman screams. The car at the order mike honks.

Cydney swings her right hand to the window pull and slams it shut.

Again, "I wanna talk to the manager." This time, with the window closed, the woman might as well be in a box. Cydney takes the bag of Deluxes and fries and shoves them in garbage, where the plastic-lidded drinks go too.

She doesn't bother with Nuts-o now. She yanks free the headset, jerking the cord from the belt transmitter, not caring if it breaks. She rushes by Marin, who walks over, concern in her face.

Cydney runs, head forward, trying to pull loose the Velcro for the transmitter, which she does. At the lockers, her face feels flush. Leaves the transmitter on the bench. Grabs her purse. Grabs her anorak. Throws the Boss Burger paper cap anywhere. Sidesteps Marin. Goes again through the public area and makes for the door. Jason kneels by a table talking to some woman he must know. Jason's eyes cut to capless Cydney, then he returns to talking to his girlfriend or whatever she is.

Outside the air cools her face.

Her heart beats like bongos. She checks inside Boss Burger, detached as anyone who's blown up a bridge, sees the head of Jason. He's hard at work. He's still kneeling, chatting up what must be his best chance for a girlfriend.

She walks a few steps and stops. She's gotta get away. But where to? It's only seven. Her mom was going to pick her up at nine.

She takes her cell phone out. How can she explain that awful woman? She slips it back in her purse.

She'll take the bus home.

The bus grinds up Weidler, going past wHEELwORX, a skateboard shop in this funky Old Portland-style house. She bites her lip. That's where I should apply. Not gonna pay less than Boss Burger and besides I can work the till. Yes. Skate punks, my hair, gotta happen.

Next afternoon, Cydney's inside wHEELwORX.

She tugs a lock of her Flamingo Pink, getting the eye of this guy in cutoffs, who straightens up some skateboards on display. "Can I help you?" he asks.

"Yes, the manager here? I wanna apply for a job."

Todd, the store manager, comes out from in back and is one smooth dude. Cydney sees him riding a skateboard like some wide-winged hawk in flight. His head is shaved bald.

"So you can sell?" he says, the gray eyes steady on Cydney like, This is your interview and it's right now.

"Yes. I think it would be so *cool* to work here." Cydney prays she is not sounding too eager and, would it be, uncool?

"You got good timing." Todd checks out approvingly—Cydney's positive—her neon locks. "I need someone twenty hours a week. You ever work with a cash register?"

"As a matter of fact, I've been working at Boss Burger, take orders, make change, all that cash register stuff."

Todd picks up a skateboard from the display beside him and spins a wheel with his thumb. "That's tight."

Her heart skips. Tomorrow after school, she'll be working here. She can see it now. And that MiniDisc, in four weeks, follows.

"Boss Burger, down on Broadway?" he asks.

Cydney nods.

"So how long you been there?"

"You want the swear-to-God truth?" Cydney says, now less sure she should have mentioned Boss Burger. Her stomach sinks.

Todd rocks his bald head once, thumb-spins the skateboard wheel again.

"Day and a half. I left."

Todd unslouches like he's getting close to knowing something. "You weren't fired?"

"No, I quit." Cydney ruffles her hair that is now *so* short.

"What happened?"

"Basically, I mean you had to been there, understand it." His gray eyes fix on her. "I flipped off a customer at the drive-up window."

"You flipped off a customer?" His eyes widen.

"She was abusive. She had to know she can't be disrespectful of people, no reason at all."

He turns to the other guy, who leans against the wall by the cash register, leafs through some skateboard magazine. "You hear that, Shane, she says she flipped off a customer at Boss Burger."

Cydney bites her lip. You'd think I'm like telling Mom all this. Pleeeeease!

"Wish I'd saw that." Shane answers in a monotone like he's lost with a photograph in the magazine.

"Whoa," Todd says, turning back to Cydney. "That was some totally committed thing to do. You understand we don't do that here, okay?"

"Sure," she says in a voice that's anything but sure.

"Well, some skaters can be a little raw. I just want you to know that. So, you done much skating?"

"You want the truth, don't you?"

Todd nods.

"Never been on a skateboard in my life, but I could learn."

His eyebrows jump like he's been shoveled one lame promise. "So you wouldn't know an ollie from a tick-tack?"

"No," she says in the unsure voice again.

"Maybe that's why we haven't had a chick working here. Though I think you could sell," Todd says. "Here, why don't you write down your name and number, so we can be in touch. Shane and I have to talk things over, see how we'd work in someone new. Okay?"

Cydney knows she's being blown off. She can see it in how Shane is burying his head in the magazine, not looking up at her to make eye contact. He knows he'll never see her working in the store, otherwise he'd be looking up, smiling. She knows she's lost. She writes on the piece of paper Todd gives her, changing the last digit of her phone number. What difference does it make anyway? He won't call.

Before she knows it, Cydney is back out on the sidewalk, ready to catch a bus. She looks back at wHEELwORX one last time, sees that it is not *that* cool.

Cydney bites her lip. So many places to work are horrible and I don't fit in.

She crosses the street for the bus shelter and notices a band poster stapled to a telephone pole. She forgets about being bummed by Todd and wHEELwORX in a hot half-sec. This is as real as it can get. It says 'Possum will play the Rose Garden. First time ever.

Later that evening, Cydney's on chat:

cydney89: i tell u i saw a poster possum's 2b at the rose garden (hyperventilates).

zoewhat: u going???

cydney89: 1st 1 2 buy tix. i'll buy 1 4 u 2.

zoewhat: u don't have a job anymore :-(.

cydney89: e-z. i get $50 this sat. & mom gives me a $30 advance on next week (smiles).

zoewhat: that's really kewl of you.

cydney89: call me ms. kewl. i really need a job now.

zoewhat: & you need to buy a minidisc . . .

cydney89: if i had my minidisc, i could tape the whole concert (long sigh).

zoewhat: & put it out 2 the net.

cydney89: 2 right.

Next afternoon, Cydney heads for Lloyd Center to apply for a job at the hair color place. She's not sure if people there are *cool*, but they're probably not like Todd at wHEELwORX: Cool on the outside, sure, but too full of himself on the inside.

She's off the bus, right in front of, what else, Boss Burger.

"Hey, Pinkie." a voice behind calls.

She turns. It's Marin.

"What happened the other night? You just left."

"A customer just got to me and I freaked," Cydney says, amazed that Marin is talking to her after her, well, *uncool* exit.

"Jason didn't know what happened. So he grills me."

"What'd you say?"

"I said you had to run home, family emergency, your mom was in the hospital. I had to make up something."

"But what about that crazy woman at the drive-up?"

"What woman?" Marin's face is blank. Blank like, A woman with tobacco-stained teeth really yelled to see the manager?

"I wonder, I wonder if that woman just drove off." Cydney feels a flush of pleasure spread across her back. Like she truly found a hall pass when she needed one. "I need to talk to Jason," Cydney tells Marin, whom she silently thanks for the second chance.

"So your mom is okay, I didn't jinx her?" Marin laughs.

"**I** want my job back, if I can still have it," Cydney tells Jason. They're back by the kitchen door and he leans, a hand on the wall.

"You know, you don't have any more chances with me, that taking off without telling anyone."

"I know, I know, I lost my head when my dad called."

"Your mom okay?"

"Yeah," Cydney says, looking into the kitchen area, seeing Armando slit open a bag of fries. "It was something that came on sudden, something she ate they said, but she's fine now." Cydney can't think of what else to say, tries to play it straight about the idea of bad food.

"Well, I'm giving you your job back, but you need to work right now, okay? I don't have time to pull out apps and call people."

"I will do better, I think I learned something."

"Okay," Jason says, looking at a loss for words, evidently wondering if he missed something.

Cydney's ready. But first, she has to call Mom for a ride at nine. Then it's all about money. Money for 'Possum tix. Money for the MiniDisc. She can record the whole concert.

Five minutes later, Cydney's at the drive-up window. Jason wants her there. That's okay. "Welcome to Boss Burger. What would you like to order?" Cydney says, a believer now.

Nobody, but nobody, driving up will take it away. That night—six weeks from now—lights blazing, strobes firing, 'Possum sonic-booming the Rose Garden, she and Zoe, they're right there. This order, the voice crackling in her headset, could be another woman with tobacco-stained teeth wanting three custom Boss Burgers. Whatever. If so, she calls Jason, tells him, *Stop talking with your girlfriend on company time. Deal with this.*

Cydney now knows the woman only wanted three burgers her way and Cydney's not giving up a 'Possum concert and a MiniDisc to record their concert for *that*.

"You want fries?" Cydney says, starting to key in the order.

ESPRESSO'D

Nelse lists in the leathered bucket seat and sets aside the commuter mug of his usual, a *caffè latte doppio* that steams. He takes a cell phone and punches numbers for the Espresso'd coffee bar he just left. What's closer to a ten on the start of a day than this? Top-down weather and across fifteen feet of pedestrian walkway from the parked Alfa, behind the glass sheet fronting Espresso'd, something in the form of woman moves with a hypnotic liquidity that's escaped every sculptor who ever lived. She's brushing crumbs, picking up napkins—all that—from tables and counters inside.

    Any other morning, Nelse would have already been cubicle-bound to Conifer Logic. Today, however, one of the other woman employees called her by name, CaraJo. The revelation snagged him. Why not? Where there's a technology, there's a way.

    Nelse wordlessly thanks the gods for this technological gift that now summons CaraJo away from the window. Not that he didn't enjoy the front and side views of CaraJo at her cleaning chores, he simply also appreciates a mathematical aesthetic as she turns away—for her sacral concavity reverse-curves flawlessly to the muscular convexity of her bum as with divine motion she goes for the phone on the back wall.

    CaraJo comes on the phone with an incredibly up voice. In profile, hand on hip, leaning on the wall, she says she doesn't know any Nelse and doesn't understand what he means, he is watching her.

"I'm over here. The Alfa out front, see me?" Nelse straightens up in the bucket seat, certain that taller must be better with CaraJo.

She swivels her shoulders against the wall and looks right at him, squinting. A bit of a pause. Nelse decides her cheekbones are right up there with Lauren Hutton. Finally, she asks, "What's with the sunglasses?" She takes forefinger away from chin. "Are you some albino with red eyes?"

Nelse pulls off the Serengeti's. "That better?" CaraJo smiles nonstop and a novel warm glow surprises Nelse, thrills his back.

CaraJo tilts her head up, the cheekbones wondrous in sharper relief, and says she doesn't know that she likes this, talking on the phone to someone who's watching her. She thinks it's kind of voyeuristic. Nelse loves the up voice, its athletic breathiness. He's got an easy guess on what it might predict for her overall physical appetites.

"I have to talk with you," he says. "Tell me, can you stand another friend in your life?" She plays with errant blonde hair wisping into her eyes. Nelse beams.

A long pause. CaraJo's eyes level at his, then she gazes away. Sotto voce (Nelse is sure this woman is a seductress par excellence), she asks how would she know him from an artist's sketch on *Crime Busters*. She toes one shoe on the floor.

"You're getting the wrong idea," Nelse says, head forward with the cell phone. "I am an okay guy. Stop by every morning for a skinny latte before work. I work with computers all day and I'm just lonely. Have mercy, CaraJo."

How did he get her name, she fires back, suggesting she's not easy and might be as quick as a fighter pilot in blasting guys out of the sky.

"You looked like a CaraJo." Nelse swings the Serengeti's by an open stem.

Another pause. CaraJo smoothes blonde locks with her free hand and says in rushed words that she'd like to talk more, but it's busy and she needs to get to work.

"Same here," he says. "Be by tomorrow." CaraJo hangs up.

Next morning, early, Nelse is back. It's before 6:30 and the lights in Espresso'd aren't even on; the place is not open for business yet, a fact that doesn't faze him. He shifts on the firm bolster of the bucket seat, catching glimpses of CaraJo's blondeness. Gracefully, she darts about, readying things behind the dusky store glass in silence. He could be watching a bright tropical fish circumnavigate an aquarium. His side of the glass, a handful of coffee addicts artfully ignore each other while keeping their places by the locked door. Nelse can wait on the coffee.

He cradles the cell phone in his left hand, speed-dialing the Espresso'd number he just programmed. A quick chat with CaraJo. Who knows?—maybe an advance order.

The impressively slim cell phone stutters out beeps and Nelse yields to maxed-out anticipation: He takes a deep breath. She's gotta move, pick up the phone on the back wall.

A female voice, synthesized, comes online: "I'm sorry. The number you reached is not accepting calls from—" A ripe pause and then, "5-5-5-0-9-3-1," which Nelse, shocked, must accept as his number. The other side of the glass, CaraJo floats about her chores, does not miss a beat.

"Please hang up your receiver and feel free to contact our offices during normal business hours for more information. Thank you."

He bites his bottom lip. Geez, Louise. Why'd she block my number? He folds the cell phone in two clicks and belt-clips it. She moves now in a fluorescent-lit interior.

Minutes dissolve as he gathers clues. Does she start the shift pulling barista duty or working the till? The register's his bet as she comes to the front door and gives the lock a determined twist. No complete laggard for caffeine shots, he's out of the Alfa, a Pier 1 bag in hand.

Soon enough, he's at the register, sliding a skinny *latte doppio* on the counter. Hands over a five-dollar bill, drops the change—two dollars, coins—in the tip jar.

"Got something, gonna make your life a whole lot easier."

"Okay," she replies with forbearance, skepticism.

"You clean up tables, use this. One, two swipes, all it takes." A natural sponge, he explains, from the waters off Madagascar. "Forget those cheesy sponges they make you use here."

"Anything else?" Poised and undeflected, CaraJo glances at the customer to Nelse's right.

"Yeah, when do we get together?"

"Why?"

"Our talk, you know, yesterday. Give it any more thought?"

"Listen, this is work, I'll talk to you in a min." Her fingers dance at the register keys, ready to rack up the next sale.

Nelse sits down, sips. He has to tell her he wants to bring his camera, photograph her, get that glamour on film. She didn't say no. He feels good, optimistic.

He's right. A few minutes later, CaraJo hurriedly sits beside him saying, "Gotta tell you, first time out with a guy, I only do lunch."

This is no auditory hallucination. These are true words. At this moment, he wouldn't think of leaving the table for anyone less than, say, Elle MacPherson. "Just a short, quick lunch for me, huh?" He wants to act like his pride is wounded, but he fails. He chuckles at how everything has worked out just as he planned.

"Don't laugh. You're lucky. I used to keep it to coffee breaks, but that, that was too much like work."

This latter admission Nelse takes as proof of her irrepressible humor. And with her looks, what more could he want in a woman? He remembers the camera, the quest to photograph her perfection. "Yeah, a coffee break should be a coffee break. Say, I'll bring my camera, document it all, this lunch will live in my memory forever."

CaraJo is out of the chair, her eyes agitated at new customers coming in. "Take pictures, do whatever. Remember, I can only fit lunch in my schedule."

Like that, she's back working the till, and Nelse, with no small contentment, turns his coffee cup in small increments and mentally flashes on a scene.

He drinking in CaraJo's beauty, the two of them outdoors at a round, enamelled metal table, which sprouts a sun umbrella, the Espresso'd logo writ large in white on each of its six dark-olive canvas panels. The two of them savoring the delicacies he brought: warm baguette and Brie and salmon pâté and caviar—lots of choices—and finishing with in season strawberry shortcake washed down with Espresso'd coffee, the latter, natch, to claim the table. And Evian water—it would all fit in the wicker basket, china and silverware too.

He gets up, walks over to CaraJo. "Tomorrow," he says.

"Sure, make it one-ish, after the noon-hour rush," she says with a hint of, Is it enthusiasm?

His thumb and forefinger meet in the rabbit-eared *O* of an okay sign and he is outbound, commuter mug of skinny latte in hand, sure that he's a Nick for the New Millennium and that he's found his Nora.

Next day, he's at Espresso'd, prompt as an electric bill. CaraJo assures him they're on for lunch. She's got the edge of excitement in her voice and Nelse feels at that moment he's the luckiest guy ever born.

Hours later, he's back in the passion-stirring aromas of the store and not seeing CaraJo, he inquires of another woman who cleans tables, an angular woman with a crew cut he finds attractive for some reason lost on him: "CaraJo around?"

"Sure, wait a minute. Oh, there she is—"

CaraJo emerges, really emerges, looking for all the world like a caterpillar seconds post-cocoon. She's got on a billowy, orange-white striped clown suit that's hidden somewhere the irresistible bod that was CaraJo from her ankles to the ruffled collar about her neck. Nelse gapes in disbelief.

"Recognize me?" she says, smiling with these outsized red lips on a white face with a red rubber ball of a nose stuck in the middle of it. Nelse is all the more stunned that this oddest person in the room is actually speaking to him. He wants to leave right now, chalk it up as a bad dream, come back tomorrow. Did he have the wrong day?

And worst of all she asks this in a loud voice, chewing gum the whole time. Nelse stands there like the lamest of lame dates holding a picnic basket from which, they're sharing lunch? He might as well break bread with a yak for all the companionship potential he sees here.

"Yeah, your nose gave you away," he says, trying to act nonchalant about CaraJo's shocking sartorial feat.

"If you're wondering, what the?—it's Friday afternoon. I take off early for my public service project at St. John's. Visit kids in the cancer ward. They're in love with me." She says this, jaws flapping away with a real wad of gum. Nelse would bet anything she's lying about the kids with cancer, but would she go and rent a costume just to make him out as a fool? He doesn't really know and suggests they sit outside at one of the umbrellaed tables.

"That's commendable," he says. "Just commendable."

"I try."

He wants to see CaraJo the way she used to be. He decides if he's going to take pictures, she'd look better without that ridiculous red nose on her face. "Wanna do me a favor?" he asks.

"What's that?"

"Give that nose a rest while we eat. I wanna see the real you, not some bank-robber disguise."

"Forget it. This is good enough for my kids, it's good enough for you."

The next few minutes at the table are awkward. He has to open the wicker picnic basket that now seems a bit out of place with CaraJo the Clown, who looks more like she wants to eat something from McDonald's, not the herbed pasta salad that he's putting out on faux china plates.

"You went to so much trouble," CaraJo says, following with a run of fast chews on her wad of gum like she's about to pull its salivaed pinkness from her mouth and stick it on the plate, which she does. He's almost lost his appetite as he opens and hands her an Evian, an inverted plastic cup hanging on the bottle neck.

Then his PalmPilot starts beeping in his shirt pocket, which he extracts to read ASK CARAJO IF SHE WANTS TO GO TO ART MUSEUM SUNDAY AFTERNOON, a reminder he could do without if she's taken to wearing this sexless habit of parachute clothes. He presses the Clear button.

But it's really that red bulbous nose that destroys all the beauty he saw in CaraJo. That Rudolph bulb mocks his attraction to her. He must focus on getting food on the table. She slivers off some of the resilient Brie, attaching it to a cracker. "You did too much. I feel like I'm in Masterpiece Theatre, china plates and all."

Nelse wants to say, "Why did I bother?" and instead keeps mum, slathering the pinkish salmon pâté—which CaraJo ignores—on a baguette slice, then bites, chews, and swallows with a new dryness in his throat.

Again, Nelse remembers the camera he stuffed in the wicker basket. "Hey, I wanna take your picture." He does a quick checkout of his point-and-shoot.

"Sure, me eating or not?"

"Doesn't matter," he says, framing CaraJo in the viewfinder, unable to ignore the something in the picture that's really wrong. "Now, one thing, the nose—" His free hand motions, withdrawing a cupped-finger mask from his face, emphatically swiveling his wrist down, and planting his phantom nose flat on the table.

"Try living with it." Her smirk is nearly lost in all the makeup.

"No, I gotta recognize you as you." It's bad enough that she has white smeared all over her face, black matting out those delicate eyebrows, and red burlesquing what he remembered as sexy lips. That plumber's helper of a nose has got to go.

"Sorry. You're gonna have to remember me this way. Take your silly picture."

Nelse's arms feel heavy as if he can't bear holding the camera anymore, can't push the button and take the first picture. Besides, any shot he'd take would only be a prickly reminder that CaraJo was making a joke of his desire for her. Living on in glossy color, her image would tease him. She'd be forever ready to leave and tell her fellow workers every last detail of how he reacted when she took out that wad of gum and stuck it to the plate he'd so carefully handed her. He knows that for her it's a game where she can break the rules and beat him every time only because he follows the rules like religion.

His PalmPilot starts beeping again. He can't take it out—he's holding the camera and besides, his arms are still sluggish. It keeps beeping.

"Can't you shut that off? It drives me ca-*ray*-zy," she says, laughing.

"Doesn't bother me," he says without apology.

"Here, you need help—" CaraJo reaches toward him in the viewfinder, toward his pocket and the electronic marvel that he mail-ordered for $399, no tax to Oregon buyers. His snapshot-composing eye goes unfocussed. She touches it, she'll drop it, drop it on the ground.

Then suddenly, his arms alive, the camera on the table, his hand at her face, a deeply satisfying wrench, and the rubber bulb, separate from her nose, bounces on the cement.

Her face is nothing but a shock of disbelief and a naked nose lost in makeup.

He picks up his camera because the CaraJo he dreamt about the last few days is recognizable, sorta. He needs these pictures.

Her face is no-mercies-offered, no-prisoners-taken resolve. She picks up her cup of coffee and flings liquid content, a fact he sees coming through the viewfinder.

The camera lens goes watery, his face stings from the burning liquid, and for humiliation in good measure, he doesn't get off a shot. His white shirt is now splotchy brown, reeks of coffee, and is wet.

CaraJo stands abruptly in her clown suit—before he can even say an angry word—knocks the plastic chair over, wads her napkin, throws it violently at the table, and walks away, leaving no more target than her billowy, striped back slipping inside the glass door for him to hurl an epithet. It's no use. She's inside Espresso'd so quickly, she wouldn't hear him anyway. Wouldn't hear him utter the word *bitch* that stays frozen in his throat.

He stands there, camera in hand, wiping his face dry with his shirt sleeve that's also wet, not sure what to think, there is so much to think about. Like the fishy aftertaste in his mouth. He drinks what's left of the Evian water in his glass that amazingly was not spilled in the commotion.

He's not sure what to do next. He gives the table one drill of a stare. The circular metal tabletop is a big wasteland of defeat and there is no way he's going to bother with CaraJo anymore. He only wanted a few pictures. Apparently, that was enough to send her over the edge.

Can he help it if she's not comfortable with her looks? Great exterior, but inside, nuts-o. Away from the table, on the sidewalk, lies the silly rubber nose. He would laugh, except he's afraid tears lurk in his eyes. And there is the question of this mess.

He picks up the plate she'd been using, to put it away in the wicker basket and sees her inside sponging off a table, not using the large sponge he gave her. Which is fine. She can do it the hard way and learn.

She studiously avoids looking his way, giving the table a vigorous rubbing. Of course, she'll have to clean off the sidewalk tables soon. That's routine. Even clean off this table. It's not good for business to let messes like this sit around.

He doesn't put the plate in the wicker basket, just feels its heft. He straightens up, stands a bit taller; his shoulders shift back. He takes a relaxed breath and, intuitive click, knows how to make the best of a bad, bad situation.

Most everything on the table is just food to be thrown away. And the wicker basket, the two plates that look like china but are not, the flatware, the linen napkins—all less than forty dollars at Pier 1. He decides to consider it an expense, an expense he'd spend anyway on his next date with CaraJo, which will never happen now. Why not be rid of it? With its baggage of nuts-o CaraJo reminders, it's all unclean. Yeah.

He rattles car keys in his pocket.

He walks away from the table, clutching his camera, leaving the mess for babe CaraJo to pick up.

He thinks to sit in his Alfa and, with patient satisfaction, wait for her to clean up the table. Then take a picture of the babe in her clown suit.

She, with her piddling sponge, first having to fill half a trash can with the table leavings. Perhaps retrieve and refix that silly rubber ball. He, from a safe distance, would snap off shots without comment, of course, with just enthused camera clicks as he'd circle and kneel to shoot her from all possible angles. And the darkroom joy of selecting the best picture. Maybe blow it up and give it a caption, FIRST DATE AFTERMATH.

He fires up the Alfa, deciding against that idea. He's no sadist. Besides, he doesn't have time for cat-and-mouse waiting games.

He pauses at parking lot's edge, scans with readiness the oncoming traffic for the merge possibilities, and feels oddly giddy at how well he quit his Espresso'd habit.

He makes his move into traffic, the car picks up speed smartly, and the rush of strong Italian horses eases him against the leathered bucket seat. He has only one question on his mind as he drives back to his place to get a clean, dry shirt. Where is he going for coffee tomorrow?

STEPS

Like a number sequence—one, two, one, two, one, two—her footfalls echoed on the refinished, bare floor of the empty parlor. A parlor—this was, after all, the Arts and Crafts bungalow, for which Marsha Ngo had moments before written a personal check. Earnest money. One thousand dollars. Check in hand, Kyla, the pert, but businesslike, real estate agent who had shown Ngo the place this second time, went out to her yellow Saab curbside.

One, two, one, two. Ngo toyed with the ballpoint pen held crosswise at her lips. Have I signed my life away? Now I write check every month for thirty years, three hundred sixty times?

In a way, she had no choice about this serious purchase. Last year, newly hired by Oxford Life downtown, Ngo was looking at more bankable wealth than anyone in her family—nearly fifteen years in Oregon—dreamed possible.

And at five-seven—only teenage Jeff was taller in the family—she now had the checking account balance, she now had the credit limits to go with her commanding stature. And with no one for her to support, no dependents—young, old, or otherwise—Duc Le, the family accountant in Rose City, earlier in the year had said, "Buy a house. You must, for goodness's sake. Taxes, they eat you alive." Not one to drop sound advice, Ngo got busy on a plan of action.

The trunk lid of the Saab levered up and Kyla bent over as if on a search. Ngo thumb-clicked the ballpoint pen and—one, two—studied the heavy cove moldings around the cream, nubbly plaster ceiling. Yes, she had found the place like any number-hungry actuary would. In awry, curling photocopies of the last U.S. Census she made at the main library. Census Tract 1.01 through Census Tract 33.07, the whole city of Portland—all of it, she boiled down to a time-well-spent spreadsheet in Excel.

For that was how the Irvington Neighborhood, and then this place on NE 23rd, came up: strong educational levels, good incomes, and big plus, high homeownership rates. Ngo stopped the deliberate pacing, took a deep breath. After the numbers were crunched and especially after Kyla said, "Irvington, good choice. Definitely the hot market right now," Ngo knew she was on the right path.

Kyla's frothy ash-blond locks, so unlike her own dark, lank hair, reappeared in the beveled-glass panes of the front door that now eased open. "Normally, this is something I do in the office with everything in front of me." Kyla waved a blue slip of paper. "Here, your receipt for the earnest money."

"I had to see it one last time, you understand?" Ngo tucked away receipt and pen in her purse.

"Big decision, Marsha. You're not some couple, can't blame the other guy, you change your mind."

"So next is what?"

"I have a three o'clock with the sellers, their agent. I present your offer." In her light tweed suit with ruffled blouse, Kyla was the all-American matron, successful, professional. Ngo knew if anyone could make the case for the offer, three-percent off asking price, it was this woman. "We cross our fingers."

They left and a ways down the walk, Ngo turned. Two tapered, panelled columns framed the front door. The Thirty-ish front stoop exuded real character. Matching columns, two eyebrow dormers pushed up from the roofline. Ngo brought forefinger to cheekbone. Logic. Symmetry. Descartes, the Great Rationalist himself, would like this.

"You ready to move in?" Kyla said.

"Yes, but I won't sleep until I know it happened."

A few hectic weeks later, Ngo was, indeed, moved, the spacious bungalow housing what now seemed her meager belongings. A futon-style single bed. A refrigerator. A threadbare sofa needing a Salvation Army call for pickup soon. The affordable dining set from Metro Liquidators. Three folding director's chairs. Countless boxes of stuff. Two wall-shelving units accompanied by too many boxed books. And a new Dell laptop.

One weekday night, Ngo was reading, with difficulty, the latest morbidity reports from the office. She was also dozing off. The morbidity stats would have to keep. She sighed and headed up to the bedroom with the futon.

She swung open the dormer window that suggested an ellipse halved, then climbed in bed. Something like an urban lullaby, traffic hummed on distant streets. October breezes played across her face. The night air was good, like a draft of heady liquor. Her eyes, the smooth Asian lids, closed. She was fast asleep.

Then suddenly, sitting up, eyes open. Where am I? Doorbell ringing, red, blurred clock digits on window sill, *3:19*. *3:19*! What is this?

They break in—they think I'm not here.

Ngo, back bolt-erect, knew something had to be done, slid off the futon, rushed down to the parlor, the front door.

The other side, in windowed gauzy porchlight, a black man she had no reason to meet loomed. Large enough to break the door down leaning on it. Her back went shivery, her legs, concrete. Could she say anything? Was he ready to kick in? The black man's head lurched back on his thick neck.

"What *is* it?" she said.

"Is John here?" The eyes, so yellowed and bloodshot, blinked in the overhead porchlight.

"No." Right of the door windows, she held to the cold doorknob. Would mere words stop this tank of a man from crashing in? She was about to say, *I call the police*, when he turned and left and out on the sidewalk, leaves whished and the bulky figure shuffled away into a relief that was darkness.

Ngo went to go upstairs, then stopped, sat down at the first landing, her heart caught up in palpitation. Really, she was by herself. In the new place for what? Second week, third day? Her back shivered again.

Next Sunday evening Ngo visited, a few miles away, her parents for the weekly family dinner. Grilled meatballs, Saigon-style, *thịt nướng chả* with fish sauce, a culinary favorite of the Ngos and many other Vietnamese families in the Rose City Neighborhood.

With Dad's jokes and the laughter, the feasting stretched out until he and Jeff, the young Ngo still at home, excused themselves for Blazers on cable. Ngo and Mom got busy on their own shared ritual, the dishes.

"So, Marsha," she said above the watery hiss of the faucet. "Now you in a big house, bigger than house here, you all by yourself, yeah?"

"It'll be fine, plenty of room, yes." Ngo opened the dishwasher, ready for her mom's washings. Washed, coincidentally, in the same order they were to be stacked. Bowls on top.

"You, small apartment, one-room, okay, but you, big house, too many rooms, all that space, empty, make you feel more lonely, I'm afraid."

"No, mother, I'll be fine." Her mother sudsed and scrubbed the *một cái bát*, the big serving bowl and Ngo waited for more to load. "Maybe at first it was different," Ngo continued. "But I'm now used to the extra space."

"You busy with your job, yeah. I know you not like talk about it, but you meet good man, the two of you in that house, just right start a family, yeah." Her mom rushed the last words like water, as if the sentiment was not new.

"Mother!" Ngo scowled. A mosquito. She will never quit. Nothing's enough for her. Means nothing I'm an actuary. She would talk all the time marriage, she only knew about that burglar.

"I know before we talk about this. You now twenty-eight, older than I first bring it up. I have Chinh I only eighteen, okay, ten years younger from you. I think about house, big, empty, and Marsha, little, alone, there. I think she not put off family business much longer, yeah."

Ngo had to change the subject.

"Mother, listen, I'll buy a dog."

"You do that why?"

"Because I'm lonely." Lonely little Marsha, big house: It was what her mom wanted to hear. In truth, a dog was better than a burglar alarm in many ways.

"Dog okay. Just remember, another mouth to feed. Buy one small, you not go broke."

"Yes, mother."

Tomorrow was Monday. The pointed words were said, not really answered, if they ever would be. Only a few more dishes for the dishwasher that would gurgle, filling with hot water. Ngo could soon check off her Sunday duty and leave.

"**H**ey, what we got here is a fourth-down software punt." Nelse, the account service guy from Conifer Logic, was in Ngo's office. On her PC, he was demo'ing some new features of the beta software that would do everything, he said, including dice and chop mortality experience. "But I expected that."

Ngo did not know what to make of irreverent Nelse. Not unhandsome Western features, blond, chestnut eyes, some style—for a supposed geek—and he moved with a single guy's strut. And talk about American-hustle enthusiastic. He probably got up early every morning and jogged, worked up a sweat. Then on to a fast, but tasty breakfast of raisin muffin and fresh-ground coffee.

"This you expected? Haven't you finished the software?"

"There, see," Nelse said, pointing to the screen with its mere one-line message. "Got it error-trapped, sends you right back to the parameter file."

"You guys, are you giving us buggy code? We depend on you."

"No, no way. But beta is beta. We gotta keep dreaming up the crazy stuff, shake and break that code. You know, like the other day, Duncan, our FSA, says change mortality decrements to increments, see what happens."

"Mortality increments? You mean negative deaths?"

"Yeah, raising the dead from their graves. Can you see it? *Night of the Living Dead.* Population goes up because the lonesome departed get to climb out of their graves and walk around."

"You guys are so strange." The round spaniel eyes brightened, like he had relaxed and they could just keep talking.

"Nah, we just wanna make sure the program's robust. Here, this will just take seconds, reconfigures your parameter file. So what's new with you? Moved yet?"

"Oh, yes, last month."

"You like the change?" Nelse seemed about her age, she guessed, not disinterested.

"I love it, but being by myself, I decide I need a dog."

"What are you getting?"

"Wait, I remember the name right. Staffordshire bull terrier."

"Whoa, you're talking pit bull."

"Why not? Good dog for protection, no? Some guy already rung my doorbell, three in the morning."

"Your choice. But if I were you, I'd reconsider. You wanna talk unusual mortality phenomena, check out incidents with those li'l shark dogs."

"But they're lovable, so ugly and prehistoric like they walk around with dinosaurs."

"It's what they do, Marsha. Listen, call your insurance guy, ask about deductibles. Could be ten, twenty thou, cute puppy wants a sample of kiddie meat."

Ngo had to clear up this needling uncertainty about living with a pit bull, made worse by Nelse. Before noon, the next day, Ngo got her agent for the homeowner's policy, Vinh Pham, on the phone.

"Marsha, you call me why? You want to talk?" Vinh was not above joshing. He, a long-time family friend, went back to Saigon days.

Ngo said she wanted a pit bull for protection and—

"Buy the puppy, go ahead, we cover you. You in good hands. Ha, ha, ha." When visiting her parents, Vinh, more than once, would say the same thing, and turn his cupped palms over and down at the expense of his company's sloganeering.

Buy the puppy. No song by Enya ever affirmed more than Vinh's words. Ngo leaned forward. Her arm aloft, she pulled the fall of lank hair away the phone receiver cradled at her ear. She had to be sure, catch every word. "No deductible, no exclusions? I skip around the Web, see somewhere one company puts deductibles, huge, on pit bulls, Dobermans, rottweilers to cover them at all."

"I know, one company they do that, but could be for publicity more than saving any claims dollar. I never hear of a dog bite claim and I do this insurance business more than a dozen years. No, Marsha, you okay."

"That's why I called. You know, I buy a puppy I get attached."

"Yeah, you okay. You collect baseball cards, different story—"

The new software needed real scrutiny. Ngo pushed back in the desk chair. It yielded a lone squeak. By being lead actuary for software evaluation, she was in no position to let the beta report slide.

Darty pixels traced ghostlike across the PC screen. The fireworks screensaver on the Conifer ActLife insurance module seemed generic, even hokey. She hoped that irreverent Nelse's programmers had not likewise cut corners when it came to writing the code.

With steadiness, she sipped hot, puckery green tea from a white ceramic demitasse. Nelse. Maybe Nelse was only enthused, trying to make an impression, all this talk about dangerous dogs. Vinh Pham thinks otherwise and he knows liability, casualty cold. Now I do what?

I don't want a harmless toy dog, a skittery Chihuahua that runs from its shadow. Who takes them seriously? But I know anything about risk, that's what it should be. No dog-bite lawsuit ever.

Pit bull, however, it'll be sword cuts both ways. Risk of dog-bite lawsuit, but also protection perfect for me. And the lovable, ugly dog will be fun. Risk, fun. Often hard to separate.

First time I rode a moped was just like that.

A steamy afternoon, Sunday many years ago, cauliflower clouds bunch in the sky, ready for soaking downpour, will wash dusty streets of my Saigòn. Even after the take-charge Communists, we never name it Hồ Chí Minh.

I am ten years old, am playing *l'enfant perdu*, hide-and-seek, with kids outside our apartment building on Bách Nghi, down the street from Thái Sinh Market, always busy.

And up rides older cousin, Hiền, the carpenter, on a brand new moped. He beams, sitting on Honda, all shiny red and chrome. "Hoon-da, Hoon-da," he keeps saying.

I run up stairs, to get Mom, to tell her Hiền has moped. All we have is one bicycle, too big for me, to ride, when we not walk or take crowded buses. "Mommy, Hiền has a Hoon-da, a moped. He wants to take me for a ride. Can I go, Mommy?"

I run back down to street, Mom follows. This event is big. First time any of our relatives with a gasoline-powered vehicle, even two wheels.

I've never been on a moped before. I am *so* excited. Wrap my eager arms around Hiền, put my feet just right on back pegs, and hold on. Then tiny motor buzzes away below and we go fast through the street. I am almost dizzy with buildings blurring into each other before I can even see them. Bump, bump, bump. We hit the uneven cobbles with the street asphalt worn away before the corner and then wait for the cross-traffic to stop.

We go again. Fast. I pull my arms tighter around Hiền and his loose shirt flaps noisy in the wind, hits my face and stings. I don't care, I'm too happy. He goes to a corner. Tick, tick, tick, turn signal blinks orange. We don't slow at all, just lean over. I scream, I don't mean to, I just think we'll fall over, but we don't. Tiny motor buzzes away, high exhaust noise echoes off buildings, we fly past duck seller, *phở* shop on Nguyễn Bỉnh Khiêm and then another corner, we dive at a turn.

Up steep, steep hill. The one when I walk it, I'm always out of breath. The Hoon-da slows down, not too much, and I feel like we float through air without weight, like we sit on back of Most Powerful *Long* himself, the Great Dragon. I gasp and no sooner I see waters sparkling and boats like tiny toys in Saigòn River far, far below, we go down.

I hold on so, I feel Hiền's ribs under his shirt. I yell. All the way I yell because Hiền pulls me forward when he leans over the handlebars to cheat the wind. I have great fear we might have bad accident. Then we are at bottom of hill. I catch my breath and we make only a few more turns on streets that are ways I don't usually walk.

Then in front of my home, we stop. The Hoon-da motor burbles away and someone else wants a ride. I get off the back of the seat and my legs are rubbery when I try to walk and I am too happy to properly answer Mom's question, "It was exciting, no?"

The revery of old times had to end. Ngo tapped the keyboard to kill the screensaver, to get back to work. A smile of distraction snuck over her face. Yes, seeing me happy even made Mom happy then. Risk and fun. So often, together.

Ngo swiveled sideways in her desk chair, faced away from the computer monitor, let her eyelids close. Okay, I calc odds for dog bites, check out facts on insurance exclusions. Oh, I see it now. Spotty neighborhood, Southeast Portland. Many-headed dandelions in mangy lawns, every other driveway, dead, broken-window car rests on cement blocks and bricks. I push doorbell lit up beside the aluminum screen door. I'm here to talk business with the occupant, a commercial breeder of Staffordshire bull terriers.

Ngo was not convinced this aerobic morning jog with puppy Spike would work.

He was the pit bull Ngo bought, abandoning all reservation. Squinty, piggy eyes, and white all but for a large black ink spot on his rump, he was Ngo's dog. Also the playful one in the litter, so his breeder said, and probably game for any distraction. So the question, Could Spike jog?

The bungalow's front door closed to, Ngo key-locked one-handed, her other hand away with the dog leash. The morning air was cool, not chilly.

"Spike, you ready? I'm ready."

But first, the tryout walk through the weepy, gray light, quiet but for an insistent crow overhead.

"That's good, you're a good dog."

Spike got it, knew how to amble, and flat-footed along, ten feet or so of the retractable leash out.

At the next block, however, Ngo left the sidewalk and they mashed through wet leaves banked at the street curb. Her legs felt limber and she jogged not that many steps before the short-legged puppy took off—at his other speed. Out to the end of his nylon tether. Swapped himself head for tail. No embarrassment. He started over.

"You go slower now, okay?"

With the galosh-sized puppy feet, Spike once again showed smarts and padded along. Sticking to a slow warmup pace, Ngo's Sauconys scuffed the wet street, empty, save for cars docked curbside. A vault of yellowing maples, a few scattered porch lights, and they turned right at NE 20th.

Crossing on Siskiyou ahead, another woman, thin as a rail, blue-and-black Spandex. Her blonde pony tail bobbed about. Beside her, a Doberman pinscher, also lithe and—Ngo stared in disbelief—unrestrained. The edgy Dobie caught sight of Ngo, Spike and launched their way

"Oh, this very bad," Ngo said.

"Addy, come here. Now stop," the insouciant woman said. Words that escaped the dog's attention.

Short and stocky, yet every bit as lean as the Dobie, muscular Spike was ready and growled.

Ngo tiptoed backwards, clutched the leash.

"This okay, Spike, this okay . . ."

Her heart raced.

Arms akimbo, the woman gave it another, somewhat more enthused, try: "Addy, over here, *now*— Don't worry." She raised her head as if her assurance would sail over the dog to Ngo. "She won't harm anybody."

Breathing hard with teeth bared, Spike strained to get at the menacing Doberman busy sniffing from a few feet away.

"Lady, will you get your dog?!" Ngo's arm swung with the lunges of Spike.

"Ad*dy*," the woman said with an inflection of familiarity on the dog's name. The woman squeezed a small device in her hand. Loud clicks.

The intrusive Dobie turned, left Ngo unblinking, amazed— Where could she get one of those?— and ran to Ms. Spandex. "Good girl, Addy, come here." She released the errant dog.

The tension building toward the woman crumbled. Ready to say something, Ngo let her arm with the leash relax. And her grip. And Spike knew.

He surged forward, broke free. The red plastic leash handle rattled down the street and this white stocky puppy, black mark on his rump, booked to the target.

Ngo gaped. This is happening? Then she ran, her brow clenched in worry. He bites that half-wit dog, hurts that stupid woman, it's all over. "Spike!"

She needed to catch him, to save him, to save *her*.

Then the stupidest thing happened. The woman and Dobie, sure, of course, they could outrun the puppy bearing down on them, sprinted as if lives were really on the line.

Like one heat-seeking missile, short-legged Spike turned, no hesitations, up the next street. The red plastic leash handle bopped away down the asphalt, soggy leaves given flight, and Ngo pressed on with her lung-aching best to stop the speedster.

The woman, her Dobie, both long-legged, gained a half-block lead. Then they turned right.

At Knott, the quick pair got an opening between cars almost without slowing and disappeared. Then trains of cars both ways.

Ngo bit her lip. Spike! He doesn't know about cars.

The worst happened. He kept running—no pause—between cars on Knott. One little brown car slammed on its brakes, skidded sideways, and stopped, engine-dead. The plastic leash handle banged away the other side of the street.

More cars kept Ngo from crossing. Where did Spike go?

At last, after a gray monolithic Suburban, enough of an opening to race across. She squinted. Nothing. That sound of the leash gone too. What happened? He did get hit! He's dying somewhere up there next to the gutter. Ngo's head hung down. Every step she now took was a reluctant step.

Ready for the heart-breaking news, Ngo stood bristle tense in the examining room, its claustrophobic white walls stenciled everywhere with paw prints. Dr. Benoit, lanky figure in a bluish lab coat, seemed an okay choice as the closest vet listed in the Yellow Pages.

He palmed the steel stethoscope disk against the broad chest of Spike and listened. Spike squirmed. "Airways are a bit raspy. Doesn't seem to be any distress, though. Again, what happened exactly?"

"He got away from me this morning, goes after another dog. He nearly gets hit by a car, then disappears." Ngo flailed her arm in emphasis. "I find him lying on ground, wheezing away, foam on his lips like he has trouble breathing."

"What did you do?"

"I don't do anything. I don't know what to do. So I just stay with him. Maybe fifteen minutes. He starts breathing okay and finally stands up. So I thought it okay to take him home. I carried him, he liked that, then I called you."

"Okay, mornings, pollen is usually not the problem." He had to stay firm with Spike. The determined dog wanted out; he clawed the countertop. Benoit defeated that. He buckled under Spike's front legs. Ngo smiled at the doctor's confident way. "I think we're looking at an asthma episode brought on by exercise."

"You mean Spike can't exercise?"

"No, by no means. He's simply one of those dogs that can't take hard exercise, emphasis on hard, like running."

"Walking then okay?"

"Absolutely." Benoit smoothed Spike's large head and floppy, unpricked ears, then patted his husky withers. "Gotta keep his weight down."

"So that's it. He can't run anymore with me."

"Not unless he outgrows the asthma. Fifty percent of puppies do."

"I'd hoped for a companion jogging."

"Walking companion okay?" Benoit grinned like Ngo might give up jogging for walking too.

*B*oomba, *boomba, boomba* came the heavy sounds sneaking up behind Ngo out for a leafy walk with Spike. A red Honda Civic hatchback, aggressively lowered, sporting flashy chromed wheels, stopped.

"*Chào cô,*" a male voice, passenger side, called out. Young, hoody-looking, black hair, long on top, slicked back, some of that

Vietnamese gangster style. Ngo shuddered: The bad apples of her own people. They had forgotten too much about what it meant to be Vietnamese. They wanted to be American in the wrong ways. The greeter, the driver both slumped in the car seats like they were off to a drive-by shooting. She had to ignore them.

Ngo furrowed her brow, turned away. Okay, so they guess right I'm Vietnamese, speak the language. I don't need to talk to them.

"*Chào cô*," the guy said once more, persistent. Politely ignoring them would only provoke. She glanced their way to acknowledge them. The showy car crept along and matched her steps.

"You speak Vietnamese?" the passenger asked in a thin voice. Ngo shook her head. Not to *you*. Good. They think I'm white-bread Vietnamese, only speak English. She kept walking, so did Spike. "Excuse me, Miss, you get that dog where? We like one."

Ngo arched an eyebrow at the *boomba, boomba, boomba* hip-hop duo. This is silly stuff. Spike doesn't keep bad guys away, he attracts them. Like snakes in this pocket-rocket gangster car, nothing else to do, they follow me home, I don't get rid of them.

"You sure you want pit bull, this dog very dangerous."

"Yes, pit bull, big bites." *Boomba, boomba, boomba*. The driver fussed with dash buttons for the sound system. She missed something the passenger said. "That's what we want, protect our business."

She flashed a wry smile. Business, what business? Shake down the Asian store owners, protection money? Maybe car thieves. "You have to find dog breeder," she said louder. "Don't remember name, but you can do what I did"

"What?"

She clenched Spike's leash. The dog pulled away, ready to move on. Had Spike tired of sniffing for dog dirt in the grass? "Just buy *Nickel Ads*, see under dogs. You know *Nickel Ads*?"

"Yeah, *Nickel Ads*, I know," the thin voice said clearly—the driver had now cut off the hip-hop. "People sell stuff they steal at night . . ." The black-haired slickster laughed, something he must have known nothing about.

"Get a copy, call those places that sell pit bulls."

"You pay how much?"

"One-fifty." She held fast to Spike's leash, out like a tightwire. The puppy wanted to walk and now a price on his head too? Would he understand, her needing to make this demeaning admission to lose these guys?

"Good protection, no?"

"Bites like bear trap." Ngo laughed. To look at Spike's squinty, triangular eyes, his monster mouth, how could that not be true?

"Miss, we no try him," he said, conceding, yes, Ngo had one killer dog guarding her. Spike's looks really would repel these *boomba, boomba, boomba* pests. "Gotta go to our business, do work."

"*Chào*," the driver said, speaking at last.

Boomba, boomba, boomba. They drove off, the red Civic's oversized exhaust pipe blatting away.

"So how's he doing?" Dr. Benoit asked Ngo. Once more he managed a Spike struggle at the examining table.

"Great. Every day, we walk. But he sees another dog, he's tugging on the leash." As if in sympathy, Ngo waggled her right hand. "I worry when he gets bigger, he'll break loose and run."

"Muzzles. Muzzles always work." An idea that had already hit Ngo. "So no more asthmatic attacks?"

"Not a one."

"Good. Keep walking him outside. I'll go ahead and write a prescription, something for asthma you can have just in case."

"It's funny, Spike was supposed to solve problems in my life: burglar alarm, protection when I jog—now keeping him healthy's the big challenge."

"Or one of life's little adjustments."

"I know, like buying this house. Before I worried about too much debt. Now, once a month, I write check, no big deal—" Ngo brought hand to mouth. *What am I saying?* She had caught her words, she did not say, *It will be the same with Spike.*

Benoit's right cheek tightened, a suggestion of a dimple. "Anyway, just keep," he said, "taking Spike for walks, good tonic for the heart and everything else. He'll be fine."

"**S**o, tell me, despite my good advice, you had to go get a shark dog, didn't you?" Nelse said. At Ngo's desk with more of the beta software enhancements, he loaded the CD-ROM drive and eyed the puppy in the new framed snapshot.

"Yes, nice puppy, looks very mean, he keeps bad guys away."

"Oh, sure, bad guys in a neighborhood like Irvington?" Ngo brought forefinger to cheekbone, contemplated the thick blondness, the back of Nelse's head. *What a surprise he still remembers where I live.*

"Well, sometimes they drive through," Ngo said, reluctant to admit, *Even my own people.*

"You still like your new home?"

"Oh, of course. Loads of room, for the furniture I don't have." Ngo chuckled. She wanted Nelse to think that even in a house, she, like him, did not have every material comfort yet.

"Did I tell you, have this friend, he's in the market for a home, says Irvington prices are up two percent a month now."

"I hear those figures too, makes me feel like every day I live in more of a bargain."

Nelse turned away from the monitor busy with a nonstop stream of messages about hardware initializations and fixed Ngo with a look of confession. "Say, I've gotta get my finances together, stop this living out of an apartment and get in a house before it's too late."

"Rising prices make people move, that's for sure," she said, repeating what Kyla said, the words real estate agents must live by.

"Yeah, Irvington's one place I wanna to check out."

Ngo flicked a dangly lock of hair out of her face. Nelse, he's more than computers, might be a friend, might be fun, go ahead, do it. "You know, you're ever in the neighborhood—" She studied the chestnut eyes for a reaction. "Stop by."

His face relaxed, could not stifle a fresh smile. "I will," he said, upbeat, confident. "You'll have me looking at houses in no time." The beam of enthusiasm stayed in his face.

"I'll show you where I live."

For no reason at all, or for all the reasons, Ngo, associate actuary, remembered that first thrilling moped ride in Saigon many years before.

ABOUT THE AUTHOR

Charlie Dickinson was born in Los Angeles, California. Now living in Portland, Oregon, he and Nancia share shelter with two felines rescued from their vagabond ways, Emma and Rudy. *The Cat at Light's End* is his first collection of short stories.